**'Here…'** Jake offered her a hand. **'Take it easy, though. That foot won't want much weight on it.'**

He held out his other hand as Ellie started to rise, and a heartbeat later she found herself on her feet, holding both Jake's hands.

And he wasn't letting go.

She couldn't even look away from his face. From a gaze that was holding hers with a look that made the rest of the world cease to exist. Everything seemed to coalesce. Surviving the rescue, finding their way to shelter, being rescued herself and the bond that had grown and grown today, thanks to Jake's heroism. So many powerful emotions.

His face was so close. She only had to lean a little and tilt her face up and her lips would meet his.

And, dear Lord… She could feel it happening, and no alarm bells were going to halt the process, no matter how loudly they tried to sound.

She was so close now she could feel his breath on her lips, and her eyes were drifting shut in anticipation of a kiss she wanted more than anything she could remember wanting in her life.

The sharp crackle of static from behind made her jump.

'Medic One, do you read? Ellie…are you there?'

# THE LOGAN TWINS

Twin brothers Ben and Jake Logan have each become wildly successful in their own way, and yet they're still getting into trouble together. This time it's when they're sailing off the coast of New Zealand and a massive storm hits, tearing their boat apart…

But the Logan brothers aren't beaten easily. And when they find themselves on very different shores neither of them knows just how much the storm—and the strong, irresistible women they meet in the heart of it—will change their lives for ever!

Read both books in this amazing duet!

**NINE MONTHS TO CHANGE HIS LIFE**
by Marion Lennox, June 2014

**THE MAVERICK MILLIONAIRE**
by Alison Roberts, July 2014

# THE MAVERICK MILLIONAIRE

BY
ALISON ROBERTS

Published in Great Britain 2014
by Mills & Boon, an imprint of Harlequin (UK) Limited,
Eton House, 18-24 Paradise Road, Richmond, Surrey, TW9 1SR

© 2014 Alison Roberts

ISBN: 978 0 263 24263 8

Harlequin (UK) Limited's policy is to use papers that are natural,
renewable and recyclable products and made from wood grown in
sustainable forests. The logging and manufacturing processes conform
to the legal environmental regulations of the country of origin.

Printed and bound in Great Britain
by CPI Antony Rowe, Chippenham, Wiltshire

**Alison Roberts** lives in Christchurch, New Zealand, and has written over sixty Mills & Boon® Medical Romances™. This is her debut for the Romance line.

As a qualified paramedic she has personal experience of the drama and emotion to be found in the world of medical professionals, and loves to weave stories with this rich background—especially when they can have a happy ending.

When Alison is not writing you'll find her indulging her passion for dancing or spending time with her friends (including Molly the dog) and her daughter Becky, who has grown up to become a brilliant artist. She also loves to travel, hates housework, and considers it a triumph when the flowers outnumber the weeds in her garden.

**Recent titles by Alison Roberts:**

200 HARLEY STREET: THE PROUD ITALIAN†
FROM VENICE WITH LOVE**
ALWAYS THE HERO*

†*200 Harley Street*
***The Christmas Express*
**Earthquake*

**These and other titles by Alison Roberts
are available in eBook format
from www.millsandboon.co.uk**

# CHAPTER ONE

*No.* NOT THIS TIME.

Jacob Logan was not going to let his older brother assume responsibility for sorting out the mess they were in. Not again. Not when he was still living with the scars from the last time.

Ben was only the elder by twenty minutes and their parents were long gone. Why was it so incredibly hard to break free of the beliefs that had got embedded in childhood?

But this time it was *his* turn to take charge. Yet again, it had been his bright idea that had got them into this mess and it was a doozy. So bad that it might be the only chance he ever got to look out for Ben for once.

This was more terrifying than the aftermath of their father's wrath for any childhood scrape they'd got themselves into. Worse than being in the thick of it in Afghanistan after they'd both escaped by running off to join the army. This was a life or death battle and the odds were getting higher that they weren't going to win.

There'd been warnings of possible gale-force winds yesterday and they'd known they could be in for a rough day, but nothing like this. Cyclone Lila had changed course unexpectedly overnight and dawn had broken to mountainous seas, vicious winds and driving rain that almost obliterated

visibility. The strong currents made the waves unpredict-
able, and the fleet of yachts in this Ultraswift-Round-the-
World Challenge had been caught, isolated and exposed in
the open seas east of New Zealand's north island.

They'd caught some of the stats on the radio before the
yacht had finally been crushed under a mountain of water
and they'd had to battle to get into their bubble of a life
raft. Winds of sixty-five knots and gusts up to two hundred miles per hour. Waves that towered up to fifty feet,
dwarfing even the biggest boats. Competitors were retir-
ing from the race in droves and turning to flee, but not
fast enough. Boats had overturned. Masts had snapped
like matchsticks. Mayday calls had gone out for men over-
board. Bodies had already been recovered. There were
search aircrafts out all over the place, but the only thing
the Logan brothers had heard over the sound of an angry
sea had been the deep drone of an air force Orion and that
had been a long way away.

The Southern Ocean was a big place when you were
in trouble.

They'd been drifting for hours now. Being tossed like
a cork in the huge seas.

By some miracle, they'd finally been spotted. A helicopter was overhead and a crewman was being lowered
on a winch. Jake could see the spare harness dangling.

One harness.

No way could more than one person get winched up
at a time.

And he wasn't going to go first. This weather was getting worse by the minute. What if the chopper *couldn't*
get back?

'You're going first,' he yelled over the noise of the sea
and the chopper.

'Like hell I am. You're going first.'

'No way. You're hurt. I can wait.'

The guy on the end of the winch had disappeared behind the crest of a wave. Caught by the water, he was dragged through and suddenly swinging dangerously closer. Someone was putting their life on the line here to rescue them.

'Look—it was my stupid idea to do this. I get to decide who goes first.'

He didn't have to say it out loud. It was his fault. Things that turned to custard had always been his fault.

Desperation had him yelling loud enough to be really heard as the rescuer got close enough to shove a harness into his hands. He pushed it towards Ben. Tried to wrestle him into it.

'Just do it, Ben. Put the harness on. You're going first.'

But Ben pushed it back. Tried to force Jake's arm into a loop.

'Someone's got to look out for you,' he yelled.

'I'll be okay. I can wait.'

'This isn't make-believe, Jake. It's not some blockbuster *movie*.'

'You think I don't know that?'

'I know you don't. You wouldn't know reality if it bit you. You're just like Mom.'

And now it was their rescuer yelling. Helping Ben to shove the harness onto Jake.

'There's no time for this.' Good grief…was this person risking life and limb to rescue them *female?*

Jake was still resisting. Still focused on his brother. 'What the hell is that supposed to mean?'

'She couldn't face reality. Why do you think she killed herself?'

That did it. The shock took the fight out of Jake. The harness was snapped into place.

'The chopper's full,' the rescuer yelled at Ben. 'We'll

come back for you as soon as we can.' She was clipping heavy-duty carabiners together and she put her face close to Jake's. 'Put your arms around me and hang on. Just hang on.'

He had no choice. A dip into icy water and then they were being dragged into the air. Spinning. He could see the bright orange life raft getting smaller and smaller, but he could still see his twin brother's face looking up at him. The shock of his words was morphing into something even worse. Maybe he'd never find out the truth even if he wanted to go there.

Dear God… *Ben*…

This shouldn't be happening. Would he ever see his brother again?

# CHAPTER TWO

THE WAVE WAS the last straw.

As though the adrenaline rush of the last few hours was simply being washed away as Eleanor Sutton faced the immediate prospect of drowning.

How much adrenaline could one person produce, anyway? She'd been burning it as fuel for hours as the rescue helicopter crew she was a part of had played a pivotal role in dealing with the stricken yachts caught up in this approaching storm. They'd pulled two people from a life raft and found another victim who'd had nothing more than his life jacket as protection as he rode the enormous swells of this angry sea.

Then they'd plucked a badly injured seaman from the deck of a yacht that was limping out of trouble with the broken mast that had been responsible for the crewman's head injuries. The chopper was full. Overfull, in fact, which was why Ellie had been left dangling on the winch line until they could either juggle space or get to a spot on land.

With her vantage point of being so much closer to the water as the chopper had bucketed through the menacing shark-gray sky, she'd been the one to spot the bright orange bubble of a life raft as it had crested one of the giant swells and then disappeared again. In the eerie light of a day that was far darker than it should be for the time, it had been all too easy to spot the two pale faces peering up at the potential rescue the helicopter advertised.

The helmet Ellie wore had built in headphones and a microphone that sat almost against her lips. Even in the howl of driving wind and rain and helicopter rotors, it was easy to communicate with both her pilot, Dave, and fellow paramedic, Mike.

'Life raft at nine o'clock. At least two people on board.'

'We can't take any more.' It was Dave who responded. 'We'd be over limit in weight and this wind is picking up.'

There was a warning tone in those casual last words. Dave was a brilliant pilot, but he was already finding it a challenge to fly in these conditions. Some extra weight with the approaching cyclone getting ever closer might be enough to tip the balance and put everybody in even more danger.

But they couldn't leave them behind. The full force of Cyclone Lila wouldn't be felt for a good few hours yet, but they shouldn't still be in the air as it was. All aircraft would be grounded by the time they reached land again. It was highly unlikely that this life raft would be spotted by any other boats and, even if it was, it would be impossible to effect a rescue.

If they didn't do something, they were signing the death warrants of another two people. There had already been too much carnage in this disastrous leg of the Ultraswift-Round-the-World yacht race. At least one death had been confirmed, a lot of serious injuries and there were still people unaccounted for.

'We can get one,' Ellie said desperately. 'He can ride with me on the end of the line. We're so close to land. We can drop him and try going back for the other one.'

There was a moment's silence from above. It was Mike who spoke this time.

'You really want to try that, Ellie?'

Did she? Despite the skin-tight rescue suit she was wearing under her flight suit, Ellie knew she was close to becoming hypothermic. Would her fingers work well enough to manipulate the harness and carabiner clips to attach another person to the winch safely? She was beyond exhaustion now, too, and that old back injury was aching abominably. What if the victim was terrified by this form of transport and struggled? Made them swing dangerously on the end of the line and make a safe landing virtually impossible?

But they all knew there was no choice.

'Let's give it a try, at least,' Ellie said. 'We can do that, can't we?'

And so they did, but Dave was having trouble keeping the chopper level in the buffeting winds, and the mountainous swells of the sea below were impossible to judge. Just as they got close enough to hover near the life raft, the foaming top of a wave reached over Ellie's head and she was suddenly underwater, being dragged through the icy sea like a fish on a line.

And that did it.

She wasn't under the water for very long at all, but it was one of those moments where time seemed to stand still. Where a million thoughts could coalesce into surprising clarity.

Eleanor Sutton was totally over this. She was thirty-two years old and she had a dodgy back. Three years ago this hadn't been the plan of how her life would be. She would be happily married. At home with a gorgeous baby. Working part time, teaching one of the subjects she was so good at. Aeromedical transport or emergency management maybe.

The fact that she could actually remember this so clearly was a death knell. This kind of adrenaline rush had been what had got her through the last three years when that life plan had been blown out of the water so devastatingly. Losing personal priorities due to living for the ultimate challenge of risking her life for others had been the way to move forward.

And it wasn't working any more.

If she could see all this so clearly as she was dragged through the wave and then swinging in clear air again over the life raft, Ellie knew it would never work again. She shouldn't be capable of thinking about anything other than how she was going to harness another body to her own in the teeth of the approaching cyclone and then get them both safely onto land somewhere.

This was it.

The last time she would be doing this.

She might as well make it count.

Unbelievably, the men in the life raft weren't ready to cooperate. Ellie had the harness in her hands. She shoved it towards one of them, holding it up to show where the arm loops were. The harness was taken by one of the men, but he immediately tried to pass it to the other.

'Just do it, Ben. Put the harness on. You're going first.'

But he pushed it back and there was a brief struggle as he tried to force the other man's arm into one of the loops. Too caught up arguing over who got to go first, they were getting nowhere.

'I'll be okay,' one of them was yelling. 'I can wait.'

'This isn't make-believe,' the other yelled back.

Static in her ears made Ellie wince.

'You still on the air?' Dave's voice crackled. 'That radio still working after getting wet?'

'Seems to be.' Ellie put her hand out to stop the life raft

bumping her away. It was dipping into another swell. And the men were still arguing. Good grief—had one just accused the other of being just like his *mother?*

She thought the terrifying dunk into that wave had been the final straw, but this was just too much. Ellie was going a lot further than the extra mile here, making her potentially last job as a rescue helicopter paramedic really count. She shouldn't be doing this and this lack of cooperation was putting them in a lot more danger. Suddenly Ellie was angry.

Angry with herself for endangering everybody involved in the helicopter hovering overhead.

Angry with these men who wanted to save each other instead of themselves.

Angry knowing that she had to face the future without the escape from reality that this job had provided so well for so long.

She was close enough to help shove the harness onto one of the men. To shout at them with all the energy her anger bestowed.

*'There's no time for this.'*

But they were ignoring her. 'What the hell is that supposed to mean?' one yelled.

There was another painful crackle of static in Ellie's headphones. 'What's going on?' Dave asked in her ear.

'Stand by,' Ellie snapped. She was still angry. Ready to knock some sense into these men, but whatever had been said while Dave had been making contact had changed something. The man she'd been helping to force the harness onto had gone completely still. Thankfully, Ellie's hands were working well enough to snap the clips into place and check that he was safely anchored to the winch line.

'The chopper's full,' she shouted at the other man.

'We'll come back for you as soon as we can.' She clipped the last carabiners together and put her face close to her patient's. 'Put your arms around me and hang on,' she instructed him grimly. 'Just hang on.' She knew they would have been listening to every word from above. Hopefully, they'd think the lack of reassurance she was providing was due to the tension of the situation, not the anger that was still bubbling in her veins like liquid lava.

'Take us up, Dave. Let's get out of here.'

'Ben...'

The despairing howl was whipped from Jacob Logan's lips by the force of the wind as he felt himself pulled both upwards and forwards in a violent swinging movement. It was also drowned by the stinging deluge of a combination of rain and sea spray, made all the more powerful by the increasing speed of the helicopter rotors above.

It was too painful to try and keep his eyes open. Jake squeezed them shut and kept them like that. He tightened his grip around the body attached to his by what he hoped was the super-strong webbing of the harnesses and solid metal clips. There was nothing he could do. However alien it felt, he had no choice but to put his faith in his rescuers and the fact that they knew what they were doing.

Shutting off any glimpse of the outside world confined his impressions more to what was happening internally, but it was impossible to identify a single emotion there.

Fear was certainly there in spades. Terror, more like, especially as they were spinning in sickening circles as the direction of movement changed from going up to going forward, interrupted by drops and jerks that were probably due to the turbulence the aircraft was having to deal with.

There was anger there as well. Not just because he'd

lost the fight over who got rescued first. Jake was angry at everything right now. At whoever had come up with the stupid idea of encouraging people to take their expensive luxury yachts out into dangerous seas and make the prize prestigious enough to make them risk their lives.

At the universe for dropping a cyclone onto precisely this part of the planet at exactly this time.

At fate for ripping him apart from his twin brother. The other half of himself.

But maybe that anger was directed *at* Ben, too. Why had he said such a dreadful thing about their mother? Something so unbelievable—so *huge*—it threatened to rip the brothers apart, not just physically but at a much deeper level. If what he'd said was true and he'd never told *him,* it had the potential to shatter the bond that had been between the men since they'd arrived in this world only twenty minutes apart.

Was life as he knew it about to end, whether or not he survived this dreadful day?

And there was something else in his head. Or his heart. No…this was soul-deep.

Something that echoed from childhood and had to be silenced.

Dealing with it was automatic now. Honed to a talent that had made him an international star as an adult. The ability to imagine the way a different person would handle the situation so that it would all be okay in the end.

To *become* that person for as long as he needed to.

This was a scene from a movie, then. Reality could be distorted. He was a paratrooper. This wasn't a dreadful accident. He was supposed to be here. It wasn't him being rescued, it was a girl. A very beautiful girl.

It was helpful that he knew that this stranger he had his arms wrapped around so firmly was female. Not that she felt exactly small and feminine, but he could work around that.

He'd never had this much trouble throwing the mental switches to step sideways out of reality. A big part of his brain was determined to remind him that this horrible situation was too real to avoid. That even if it was a movie, there'd be a stuntman to do this part because his insurance wouldn't cover taking this kind of a risk. But Jake fought back. If he could believe—and make countless others believe, the way he had done so far in his stellar career— didn't that make it at least a kind of reality?

He was out to save the world. The chopper would land them somewhere and he'd unclip his burden. He'd want to stay with the girl, of course, because he was desperately in love with her, but he'd have to go back into the storm. To risk his life to rescue…not his twin brother, that would be too corny. This was the black moment of the movie and he was the ultimate hero so maybe he was going back to rescue his enemy.

And, suddenly, the escape route that had worked since he'd been old enough to remember threw up a barrier so solid Jake could actually feel himself crashing against it.

Maybe Ben *was* the enemy now.

Even if it hadn't been a success, the effort of trying to catch something in the maelstrom of thoughts and emotions and turn it into something he could cope with had distracted him for however long this nightmare ride had been taking. Time was doing strange things, but it couldn't have been more than a few minutes.

Close to his head, he could hear his rescuer trying to talk to the helicopter pilot. The wind was howling like a wild animal around them and she was having to shout, even though she had a microphone against her lips. As close as he was, Jake couldn't catch every word.

Something about a light. A moon.

Was she kidding?

In even more of a fantasyland than he'd been trying to get into?

'The lighthouse,' Ellie told Dave, her words urgent. 'At five o'clock. It's Half Moon Island.'

'Roger that.' Dave's voice in her ears sounded strained. 'We're heading southeast.'

'No. The beach…'

'What beach?'

'Straight across from Half Moon Island. The end of the spit. Put us down there.'

'What? It's the middle of nowhere.'

'I know it. There's a house…'

It was hard enough to communicate through the external noise and the internal static without trying to explain. This area was Ellie's childhood stamping ground. Her grandfather had been the last lighthouse-keeper on Half Moon Island and the family's beach house was on an isolated part of the coast that looked directly out at the crescent of land they'd all loved.

The history didn't matter. It was the closest part of the mainland they could put her down and she knew they could find shelter. It was close enough, even, for them to drop their first victim and try to go back for the other one.

He still had her in a grip that made it an effort to breathe. An embrace that would have been unacceptably intimate from a stranger in any other situation. His face was close enough to her own to defy any concept of personal space but, curiously, Ellie didn't have any clear idea of what he looked like.

The hair plastered to his head looked like it would be very dark even if it was dry and it was too long for her taste for a man. The jaw was hidden beneath a growth of beard that had to be weeks old and his eyes were screwed shut so tightly they created wrinkles that probably made him look a lot older than he was.

He was big, that much she could tell. Big enough to make Ellie feel small and that was weird. At five feet ten, she had always towered over other women and many men. She'd envied the fragility and femininity of tiny women— until she'd needed to be stronger than ever. That had been when she'd finally appreciated the warrior blood that ran in her veins from generations past.

No man was ever going to make Eleanor Sutton feel small or insignificant again.

She put her mouth close enough to the man's ear to feel the icy touch of his skin.

'We're going to land on the beach. Keep your legs tucked up and let me control the impact.'

Dave did his best to bring them down slowly and Ellie did her best to try and judge the distance between them and the solid ground, but it had never been so difficult. The crashing rolls of surf kept distorting her line of sight and the wind was sending swirls of sand in both horizontal and vertical directions.

'Minus twenty…no…twenty-five…*fifteen*…' This descent was crazy. They were both going to end up with badly broken legs or worse. 'Ten… Slow it down, Dave.'

He must have done his absolute best, but the landing was hard and a stab of pain told Ellie that her ankle had turned despite the protection of her heavy boots. There was no time to do more than register a potentially serious fracture, however. She fell backwards with her patient on top of her and for a split second she was again aware of just how big and solid this man was.

And that she couldn't breathe.

But then they were flipped over and dragged a short distance in the sand. Ellie could feel it scraping the skin on her face like sandpaper. Filling her mouth as her microphone snapped off. The headphones inside her helmet were still working, but she didn't need Dave's urgent orders to know how vital it was that she unhook them both from the winch line before they were dragged any further towards the trees that edged the beach.

Before they both got killed or—worse—the line got tangled and brought the helicopter down.

Somehow she managed it. She threw the hook clear so that it didn't hit her patient as it was retracted and the helicopter gained height. Once she'd unclipped herself from this man, she could get into a clear position and they could lower the line to her again.

But it was taking too much time to unclip him. Her hands were so cold and she was shaking violently from a combination of the cold, pain and the sheer determination to get back and save the other man as quickly as possible.

He was trying to help.

'No,' Ellie shouted, spitting sand. 'Let me do it. You're making it harder.'

His hands fisted beside his face. 'You're going back, aren't you? To get Ben?'

'Yes. Just let me…' Finally, she unclipped the last carabiner and they were separated. Ellie almost fell the instant she tried to put weight on her injured ankle but somehow managed to lurch far enough away from her patient to wave both arms above her head to signal Dave. There was no point in shouting with the microphone long gone, but she did it anyway.

'Bring the line down. I'm ready.' She wouldn't need to worry about her ankle once she was airborne again. It shouldn't make it impossible to get the other man from the life raft.

'Sorry, El. Can't do it.' Dave's voice was clear in her ears. 'Wind's picking up and we've got a status one patient on board under ventilation.'

The helicopter was getting smaller rapidly. Gaining some height and heading down the coast.

'No...' Ellie yelled, waving her arms frantically. 'No-o-o...'

The man was beside her. 'What's going on?' he shouted. 'Where's he going?' He grabbed Ellie's shoulders and it felt like he was making an effort not to shake her until her teeth rattled. 'You've got to go back. For Ben.'

His face was twisted in desperation and Ellie knew her own expression was probably close to a mirror image of it.

'They won't let us. It's too dangerous.'

The man had let her go in order to wave *his* arms now. 'Come *back,*' he yelled. 'I *trusted* you, dammit...'

But the bright red helicopter was vanishing into the darkening skies. Ellie could still hear Dave.

'We've got your GPS coordinates. Someone will come as soon as this weather lifts. Get to some shelter. Your other radio should still work. We'll be in touch.' She could hear in his voice that he was hating leaving her like this. It broke all the unspoken rules that cemented a crew like this together. 'Stay safe, Ellie.'

The helicopter disappeared from view.

For what seemed a long, long time, Ellie and the rescued man simply stood on this isolated, totally deserted stretch of coastline and stared at the menacing cloud cover, dark enough to make the ocean beside them appear black. The foam of the crashing breakers was eerily white.

The man took several steps towards the wild surf. And

then he stopped and let out a howl of despair that made Ellie's spine tingle. He knew he'd lost his friend. The lump in her throat was big enough to be painful.

'I would have gone back,' she yelled above the roar of the wind and surf. 'If they'd let me.'

He came closer in two swift strides. 'I would have *stayed*,' he shouted back at her.

He was angry at *her?* For saving his life?

His words were a little muffled. Maybe she'd heard wrong. Dave was too far away for radio contact now and the communication had been one-sided anyway, thanks to the broken microphone. Ellie undid the chin strap of her helmet and pulled it off. The man was still shouting at her.

'Who gave *you* the right to decide who got rescued first?'

Ellie spat out some more sand. '*You're* lucky to be alive,' she informed him furiously. 'And if we don't find any shelter soon we'll probably both die of hypothermia and then all this would have been for nothing.' He wasn't the only one who could be unreasonably angry. 'Who gave *you* the right to put *my* life in danger?'

She didn't wait to see what effect her words might have had. Ellie turned and tried to pick out a landmark. She had to turn back and try to catch a glimpse of Half Moon Island to get any idea of which direction they needed to go. The lighthouse was well to her left so they had to go north. The beach house was in a direct line with the point of the island where the lighthouse was.

Confident now, Ellie set off up the beach. She didn't look to see whether he was following her. He could have his autonomy back as far as she was concerned. If he wanted to stay out here and die because she hadn't been able to rescue his friend then maybe that was *his* choice. She was going to survive if she could, thank you very much.

Except that she didn't get more than two steps away. Her ankle collapsed beneath her and she went down with a shout of anguish.

'What's the matter?' The man was crouched over her in an instant. 'What's happened?'

'It's my ankle. I… It might be broken.'

If he was swearing, the words were quiet enough for the wind to censor them. Ellie felt herself being picked up as if she weighed no more than one of those tiny women she'd once mistakenly envied. Now she was cradled in the arms of this big man as if she was a helpless child.

'Which way?' The words were as grim as the face of the man who uttered them.

'North.' Ellie pointed. 'About a mile.'

A gust of wind, vicious enough to make this solid man stagger, reminded her that this was only the beginning of this cyclone. Things were going to get a whole lot worse before they got any better.

The stabs of pain coming up her leg from her ankle were bad enough to make her feel sick. On top of her exhaustion and the knowledge that they were in real trouble here, it was enough to make her head spin. She couldn't faint. If she did, how would he know how to find the beach house, which was probably their only hope of surviving?

'There's a river,' she added. 'We turn inland there.'

She could feel his arms tighten around her. It had to be incredibly hard, carrying somebody as tall as she was in the face of this wind and on soft sand, and they had a long way to go.

Could he do it?

Ellie had no choice but to put her faith in him, however hard that was to do. With a groan that came more from defeat than pain, she screwed her eyes shut and buried her face against his chest as he staggered along the beach.

It had been a very long time since she had felt a man's arms around her like this.

At least she wouldn't die alone.

# CHAPTER THREE

SHE WAS NO lightweight, this woman in his arms.

Jake had to lean forward into the fierce wind and his feet were dragging in the soft sand that was no match for these conditions. It swirled around enough to obscure his feet completely and it would have reached his nose and eyes if the rain hadn't been heavy enough to drive it down again.

Another blast of wind made Jake stagger and almost fall. He gritted his teeth and battled on. They had to find shelter. She'd been right. He might wish it was Ben instead of him, but he *was* lucky to still be alive and he owed it to her to try and make sure the heroic actions of his rescuers weren't wasted to the extent that one of them lost her life.

A river, she'd said. Good grief. He didn't even know the name of the woman he was carrying. A person who had risked her life for his and he'd been ungrateful enough to practically tell her he wished she hadn't. That he would have stayed with Ben if he'd been given a choice.

His left leg was dragging more than the right and a familiar ache was tightening like a vice in his thigh.

Another vice was tightening around his heart as his thoughts were dragged back to Ben, who would still be being tossed around in the ocean in that pathetically small life raft.

The combination of his sore leg and thoughts of his brother inevitably dragged his mind back to Afghanistan. They'd only been nineteen when they'd joined the army. Sixteen years ago now but the memories were as fresh as ever. Had it been his idea first that it was the ideal way to escape their father?

Charles Logan's voice had the ability to echo in his head with all the force of the gunfire from a war zone.

*You moronic imbeciles, you're your mother's children, you've inherited nothing from me. Stupid, stupid, stupid...*

No. They'd both wanted to run. Both had needed the brutal reality of the army to find out what life was like outside an overprivileged upbringing. To find out who *they* really were.

But *he* had been more excited about it, hadn't he? In the movies, the soldiers were heroes and it always came out all right for them in the end.

They weren't supposed to get shipped home with a shattered leg as the aftermath of being collateral damage from a bus full of school kids that had been targeted by a roadside bomb.

His brother's last words still echoed in his head.

*Why do you think she killed herself?*

It *had* been Ben who'd found her, all those years ago, when the boys had been only fourteen.

Did he know something he'd never told *him?* Had he found evidence that it hadn't been an accidental overdose of prescription meds washed down with alcohol?

A *note,* even?

*No.* It couldn't be true. She wouldn't have deserted her children with such finality. She'd *loved* them, even if she hadn't been around often enough to show them how much.

A cry was ripped from Jake's lips. An anguished denial of accepting such a premeditated abandonment.

Denial, too, of what was happening right now? That his brother was out there somewhere in that merciless ocean? Too cold to hang on any longer?

Drowned already, even?

No. Surely he'd know. He'd feel it if his other half was being ripped away for eternity.

The cry of pain was enough to pull Ellie from the mental haze she'd been clinging to as she kept her face buried from the outside world, thinking of nothing more than the comfort of being held in strong arms and, hopefully, being carried to safety.

What had she been thinking? Eleanor Sutton wasn't some swooning heroine from medieval times. She didn't depend on anyone else. She could look after herself.

'Put me down,' Ellie ordered.

But he kept lurching forward into the biting wind and rain.

'No. We're not at the river.'

'I need to see where we are, then.' She twisted in his arms to look towards the sea.

Taking her helmet off had probably been a bad idea. The wind was pulling long strands from the braid that hung down over Jake's arm. They were plastered against her face the moment they came free and she had to drag them away repeatedly to try and see properly.

'I can't see it. The waves are too high.'

'See what?'

'The light from the lighthouse. The bach is in a direct line with the light, just before the river mouth.'

'The *what*?'

'The bach. A holiday house.' Ellie had finally picked up the drawl in the man's voice. 'Are you American?'

'Yep.'

'A cabin, then. Like you'd have by a lake or in the woods. Only this one's near the beach and it's the only one for a hundred miles.'

'How do you know it's even there?'

'Because I own it.' Maybe it wasn't dark enough for the automatic light to be triggered, but she'd seen it earlier, hadn't she? When she'd told Dave where to drop them?

Maybe she'd only seen the lighthouse itself and it had been childhood memories that had supplied the flash of light. The flash she'd watched for in the night since that first time she'd stayed on the island with her grandfather. A comforting presence that had assured a small girl she was safe even if she was on a tiny island in the middle of a very big sea.

'We'll have to keep going till we get to the river. I can find the way from there.'

How long did he keep struggling against the wind before they finally reached the river mouth? Long enough for Ellie to know she'd never felt this cold in her life. At least they had the wind behind them as they turned inland, but there was a new danger when they reached the forest of native bush that came to meet the coastline in this deserted area. The massive pohutukawa trees were hundreds of years old and there were any number of dead branches coming loose in the vicious wind to crash down around them. Live bits were breaking off, too, leafy enough to make it impossible to see the old track that led to the bach.

Ellie had to rely on instinct. Her fear was growing. Had she made a terrible mistake, telling Dave they could find shelter here? The little house that Grandpa and her father had built had seemed so solid, wedged into the bush that had provided the wood to make it. A part of the forest that would always be here even if she had never come back. A touchstone for her life that was a part of her soul.

But how many storms had there been in the years that had passed? Had the tiny dwelling disintegrated—like all the hugely important things in her life seemed to have a habit of doing?

No.

They almost missed it. They were off to one side of the patch of land she owned. She might have let herself get carried right past if she hadn't spotted the tiny hut that sat discreetly tucked against the twisted trunk of one of the huge pohutukawas.

'We're here,' she shouted.

The man looked at the hut. If he went inside the bleached wood of its walls, he would have to bend his head and he wouldn't be able to stretch out his arms. 'Are you *kidding* me? *That's* your cabin?'

Ellie actually laughed aloud.

'No. That's the dunny.'

'The *what?*'

'The long drop. Toilet.' Oh, yeah…he was American. 'It's the *bathroom*.'

She didn't wait to see a look of disgust about how primitive the facilities were. The track from the outhouse to the real house was overgrown, but Ellie knew exactly where she was now. And if the outhouse had survived, maybe everything else was exactly as it should be. Within a few steps they could both see the back porch of the beach house, with its neatly stacked pile of firewood. The relief of seeing it look just like it always had brought a huge lump to Ellie's throat.

She felt herself being tipped as he leaned down to grasp the battered iron knob of the door. He turned and pushed. The door rattled but didn't open.

'It's *locked*.'

She couldn't blame him for sounding shocked. It wasn't

as if another living soul was likely to come here when the only access was by boat so why would anybody bother locking it?

Another childhood memory surfaced. The door that had been purchased in a city junkyard had been roped to the deck of the yacht, along with an old couch and a pot-belly stove.

*'The door's even got a lock and a key.'* Her father had laughed. *'That'll keep the possums out.'*

A family joke that had become a tradition. Unlocking the bach meant they were in residence in their tiny patch of paradise. Locking it meant a return to reality.

'I know where the key is. Put me down.'

This time he complied and it was Ellie's turn to be shocked as she felt the loss of those secure arms around her, along with the chill of losing his body warmth that she hadn't been aware of until now. She staggered a lit-tle, but her ankle wasn't as bad as it had been. Hellishly painful but it didn't collapse completely when she tested it with a bit of weight. Maybe it was a bad sprain rather than a fracture.

'Can you walk?'

'I only need to get to the meat safe. The key's in there.'

The wire netting walls of the meat safe were mangled, probably by possums, and the box frame was hanging by only one corner, but the big, wrought-iron key was still on its rusty nail. Getting it inside the lock was a mission for her frozen hands, though, and turning it seemed im-possible.

'It must be rusty.' Ellie groaned with the effort of try-ing to turn the key.

'Let me try.' His hands covered hers and pushed her fingers away so that he could find the end of the key. She was still wearing her rescue gloves and his hands had to be a lot colder than hers were, but the pressure of the contact felt like it was skin to skin. Warm.

Maybe it was the reassurance that she wasn't alone that was so comforting?

He was shivering badly, Ellie noticed, but when he jiggled the key and then turned it, she could hear the clunk of the old lock opening.

And then they were inside and the sound of the storm was suddenly muffled.

Safety.

They might be frozen to the bone and in the middle of nowhere, but they had shelter.

Jake was safe, thanks to this woman. Thanks to her astonishing courage. She'd not only risked her life to get him out of that life raft, she'd battled the elements, despite being injured, to lead him here. To a place where they had four walls and a roof and they could survive until the storm was over.

She seemed as stunned as he was. They both stood there, staring at each other, saying nothing. It couldn't be nighttime yet, but it was dark enough in here to make it difficult to see very clearly. She was tall, Jake noted, but still a good few inches shorter than his six feet two. Eyes dark enough to look black in this light and her lips were deathly pale but still couldn't hide the lines of a generous mouth. A rope of wet hair hung over one shoulder almost as far as her waist.

'What's your name?' He'd been so used to shouting to be heard outside that his voice came out loudly enough to make her jump.

'Eleanor Sutton. Ellie.'

'I'm Jacob Logan. Jake.'

'Hi, Jake.' She was trying to smile but loosening

her facial muscles only made her shiver uncontrollably. 'P-pleased to m-meet you.'

'Likewise, Ellie.' Jake nodded instead of smiling.

His name clearly didn't mean anything to her and it was a weird feeling not to be instantly recognised. He didn't look much like himself, of course. Even his own mother probably wouldn't have recognised him in this dim light with the heavy growth of beard and the long hair he'd had to adopt for his latest movie role. But instant demotion from a megastar to a…a *nobody* was very strange.

Jake wasn't sure he liked it.

And yet it was oddly comforting. It took him back to a time when he had only been known for being 'one of those wild Logan boys.' Closer to Ben, somehow.

Should he tell her? Was it being dishonest not to? Would Ben consider this a form of play-acting as well?

Keeping silent didn't feel like acting a part. Just being the person he used to be. And there would be no reason for this Ellie to present herself as anything other than who she really was and, in Jake's experience, that wasn't something he could ever trust. This might be the only time in his life that he got to see how a stranger reacted to him as a person without the trappings of extreme wealth or fame. He was curious enough to find this almost a distraction from his desperate worry about Ben.

'We need to get warm.' She wasn't even looking at him now. 'There should be enough dry wood to get the fire and the stove going. Hopefully the possums won't have been inside. There'll be plenty of blankets on the beds. And there's kerosene lamps if the fuel hasn't evaporated or something. It's been a fair few years since I was here.'

Beds? For the first time, Jake took a good look around himself.

The dwelling was made of rustic, rough-hewn boards

that had aged to a silvery-gray that made it look like drift-wood. An antique glass-and-metal lamp hung from a butcher's hook in the ceiling and there was a collection of big shells lined with iridescent shades of blue and purple attached to the wall in a curly pattern. Beside that was a poster of a lighthouse, its beam lighting up a stormy sky while massive waves thundered onto rocks below. There was a kitchen of sorts in one corner of the square space, with a bench and a sink beside the potbelly stove close to a small wooden table and spindle-back chairs.

The other half of the space was taken up with an ancient-looking couch and an armchair, positioned in front of an open fireplace. Two doorless openings in the walls on either side of the fireplace led to dark spaces beyond. The bedrooms?

'Don't just stand there.' The authority in her voice made Jake feel like he was back at school. Or under the charge of one of the many nannies the Logan boys had terrorised. Incredibly, he had to hide a wry smile. No woman had ever spoken to him like this in his adult life. And then he re-membered being shouted at on the beach. Being told that no one would be going back to rescue his brother.

What did it matter whether Ellie knew who he was? Or what she thought of him?

Nothing would ever matter if he'd lost Ben.

Ellie was opening a cupboard in the kitchen. She pulled out a big tin. 'Do something useful. You'll get even colder if you don't move. You can get some wood in from the porch.' She prised open the lid of the tin. '*Yes*…we have matches.'

A fire. Warmth. This basic survival need drove any other thoughts from Jake's head as he obeyed the order. He took an armful of small sticks in first to act as kin-dling and then went back for the more solid lumps of wood. His brain felt as frozen as his fingers. Worry about Ben was still there along with the anger of no attempt being made to rescue him, but he couldn't even harness the energy of that anger to help him move faster. And then something scuttled away as he lifted a piece of wood. Did New Zealand have poisonous spiders, like Australia did? Or snakes?

Man, he was going to have some story to tell Ben when he saw him again.

*If* he saw him again.

There was a puddle of water on the floor where Ellie was crouching to light the fire and he could see how badly her hands were shaking, but she'd managed to arrange small sticks on a nest of paper and while the first two matches spluttered and died, the third grew into a small flame.

She looked up as he walked towards her with the wood. He saw the way her eyes widened with shock.

'You're limping.' Her tone was accusing. 'You're hurt. And I let you carry me all that way. Why didn't you *tell* me?'

'I'm not hurt.' He dumped the wood on the floor beside her. His old injury was hardly a state secret, but it wasn't something he mentioned if he could avoid it.

'I'm a paramedic, Jake. I've got eyes. I can *see*—'

'Drop it,' he growled. 'I told you. I haven't been injured. Not in the last ten years anyway.'

'Oh…' She caught her bottom lip between her teeth. Maybe she was attempting a smile. 'Old war wound, huh?'

He glared at her. 'First time anyone's found it funny.'

Her face changed. Was she embarrassed? Not that she was about to apologise. There was an awkward silence as she turned her attention back to the fire and then she must have decided that it was best ignored.

* * *

'Some rats or mice had shredded the paper for me,' Ellie said. 'Good thing, too, because my fingers are still too cold to work properly.' Her tone was deliberately lighter. Impersonal, even. 'Don't think we'll use the beds, but the blankets might be okay.'

The wood sizzled a little, but the flame was still growing. The glow caught Ellie's face as she leaned in to blow gently on the fire. Water dripped from her long braid to add to the puddle at her feet. Smoke puffed out and made her cough.

'There could well be a bird's nest or two in the chimney, but they should burn away soon. We'll get the potbelly going, too, if we can, and that should get things toasty in no time.'

Jake had to forgive the dismissal of his old injury as some kind of joke. She didn't know the truth and, if he wasn't prepared to enlighten her, it would be unfair to hold a grudge. And he had to admire her. She was capable, this Eleanor Sutton, but that was hardly surprising given what she did for a job. Jake was given the task of feeding larger sticks into the fire as it grew while Ellie limped over to the kitchen to get the stove going. His hands began aching unbearably as heat finally penetrated the frozen layer of skin and, when he looked up, he saw Ellie's pained expression as she shook her hands.

'Hurts, doesn't it?'

'It's good. Means there's some circulation happening and nerves are waking up.' She nodded in satisfaction at the fire Jake was tending. 'I'll see if I can find us some dry clothes. My dad kept a trunk of stuff under the bed and it's a tin trunk so it should have kept the rats out.'

'Do you get snakes, too?'

'No snakes in New Zealand. Have you never been here before?'

'No.'

'I guess you were just passing by with the yacht race. Wasn't there a stop planned in Auckland?'

'Yeah. I was getting off then. I'm here for a job. That was why I talked Ben into giving me a lift on his yacht.'

'Ben? That's your friend who was on the life raft with you?'

'He's my brother. Twin brother.'

'Oh…'

The enormity of having to leave Ben behind and not trying to go back and get him was clearly registering.

'I…I'm sorry, Jake.'

'Yeah… Me, too.'

'It was a good life raft. There's still hope that he'll make it.'

Jake found himself staring at Ellie. It felt very odd—his gaze clinging to hers like this. As if he was pleading…

Desperately wanting to believe.

Begging her to prove herself trustworthy?

She was in the business of rescuing people who found themselves in dire situations so she should know what she was talking about.

'We weren't the only rescue team out there,' she told him quietly. 'There were other choppers. Planes. And there's other boats. Container ships as well as the coast-guard. There's plenty of daylight left and…'

There was such compassion in her eyes and her body language. The way she was leaning towards him. Holding out one hand. If she'd been close enough, she'd be touching him right now.

He wished she was that close.

'And there are literally hundreds of islands on this part

of the coastline. All it needs is for a current to get him close to land and he'll be able to find shelter until the worst of the storm is over.'

Maybe it was the compassion he could see that did it. Or the comfort of the reassurance she was offering. Or maybe it was because of that longing that she had been close enough to underpin her words with human touch.

Whatever it was, Jake could pull back. Yes, she was offering him what he wanted more than anything in this moment. And the invitation to believe her was so sincere, but they were all like that, weren't they? Especially women.

He knew better than to trust.

'Yeah…right…' He wrenched his gaze free, turning back towards the fire and using a stick to poke at it. He didn't want to talk about Ben. He didn't want to show this stranger how he was really feeling. How *afraid* he was. Who knew what contacts she might have? What could turn up as a headline on some celebrity website?

The warmth Ellie had been getting from the stove seemed to have been shut off and the cold in her gut turned into a lead weight.

No wonder they'd been arguing about who got to be rescued first. Or that Jake had said he would have stayed if he'd been given the choice. She didn't even have a sibling and these men were twin brothers. She could imagine how close they were. As close as she'd dreamed of being with another living soul. Loving—and being loved—enough for one's own safety to not be the priority.

She would have gone back for Ben if it had been possible, but it hadn't been. At least she'd brought Jake to safety, but maybe, in the end, he wouldn't thank her for that. He obviously didn't want to talk about it. He was hunched over in front of the fire, looking very grim as he poked at the burning sticks, sending sparks flying and creating a new cloud of smoke. Fiercely shutting her out.

Was it the smoke in his eyes that made him rub at them with the heel of his hand? Even hunched up, she was aware again of what a big man he was. Intimidatingly big. She knew that trying to offer any further comfort would be unwelcome. She'd probably put her foot in it, too, the way she had when she'd tried to make some kind of joke about his obvious limp.

It had been the way Grandpa had brushed off any concern about his physical wellbeing.

*It's nothing, chicken. Just the old war wound playing up.*

But Jake was an American. Had she made a joke about some horrible injury he'd suffered in somewhere like Afghanistan? She'd been too flustered to think of a way to apologise without it seeming insincere. Or prying. There was something about this man that suggested he valued his privacy a lot more than most people.

So, once again, she simply avoided anything personal.

'I'll go and see if I can find us those dry clothes.'

By the time Ellie returned with an armload of clothes from the old tin trunk, the living area of the small house was already feeling a lot warmer.

'The trousers are pretty horrible, but we've scored with a couple of Swanndris.'

Jake looked up from where he was still crouched in front of the fire. He was shivering uncontrollably despite being so close to the heat. 'S-swan—what?'

'They're shirts. I'm wearing one.' Ellie dumped the pile she was holding onto the sofa, extracting a black-and-red-checked garment to hold out to Jake. 'New Zealand icon. A hundred percent wool. Farmers have relied on them for decades over here and they're the best thing for warmth. Even better, these ones are huge. Should fit you a treat.'

Neither her father or grandfather had been small men by any means. The shirt Ellie was wearing came well down over the baggy track pants she'd struggled into in the bedroom, but it was just as well they were so loose because they'd gone right over the sodden boots that had laces she couldn't manage to undo yet. And maybe it was better to leave them on. At least her ankle was splinted by the heavy leather and padding of her socks.

He took the shirt and nodded. 'Thanks.'

'Don't just stare at it. Put it on. No, hang on…' Ellie dived back into the pile. 'Here's a singlet that can go on first so it's not itchy.'

Getting changed into dry clothes was easier said than done. Ellie had found it enough of a struggle getting out of her wet clothes in the bedroom and she'd been wearing state-of-the-art gloves to protect her hands up until now. Jake's hands had been bare ever since he'd been plucked from the life raft and were still so cold there was no way he could manage the zipper of the heavy anorak he was wearing.

He fumbled several times, cursed softly and then stopped trying. Ellie dragged her gaze up from his fingers to his face and, for a long moment, they simply stared at each other.

The fire was crackling with some enthusiasm now. Adding enough light to the dark, stormy afternoon for her to get a good look at this man. He was big, broad shouldered and…and *wild* looking, with that long hair and the beard. His face was fierce looking anyway, with a nose that commanded attention and accentuated the shadowed eyes that had an almost hawk-like intensity.

The pull of something—an awareness that was deep

enough to be disturbing—made Ellie's mouth go dry. She tore her gaze away from those compelling eyes. They both knew she had no choice here.

'I'll help you,' she said.

Her voice sounded weird so she pressed her lips together and said nothing else as she started to help him undress. The scrape of the metal zip sounded curiously loud. He had layers underneath. A sodden woollen pullover and thermal gear beneath that.

And then there was skin. Rather a lot of skin covering the kind of torso that spoke of a great deal of physical effort.

Ripped. That was the only word for it.

Dark discs of nipples hardened by the cold decorated an almost hairless chest that seemed at odds with the amount of hair Jake favoured on his head and face.

And…dear Lord, there was a tattoo in the strangest place. A line of what looked like Chinese characters ran from his armpit to disappear into the waistband of his jeans.

It was discreet body art and it must have significance, but Ellie wasn't about to ask. She shouldn't even be looking. Just as well it got covered up as Jake pulled on the black singlet and then the thick woollen shirt. He managed to pop the button on his jeans but, again, the zipper was beyond the motor skills that had returned to his hands so far.

Ellie had undressed countless patients in her career. She'd cut through and removed clothing and exposed every inch of skin of people without the slightest personal reaction. Why did it have to be now that she was so aware of touching someone in such an intimate area? Why did she feel so uncomfortable she had to swallow hard and actually close her eyes for a heartbeat?

Like remembering her past when it should have been

totally obliterated by the adrenaline of being in real danger, maybe this was a sign that she was no longer fit for active service as a paramedic. Something like grief washed through Ellie at the thought and it was easy to turn that into a kind of anger. Impatience, anyway, to get the job over with.

'I'll do the zip,' she snapped. 'You should be able to manage the rest.'

She tried not to think of what her fingers were brushing. The zipper got stuck halfway down and she had to pull it back up and try again. A warmth that had nothing to do with the fire crept into her cheeks. As soon as she got the zipper down past where it had stuck, she dropped her hands as though the metal was red hot and she turned away as Jake hooked his thumbs into the waistband and started peeling the wet fabric from his skin.

She'd seen enough.

Too much.

Nobody had undressed Jake Logan without his invitation since he'd been about two years old and had kicked his nanny to demonstrate his desire for independence.

Except for when he'd been in the care of the army medics, of course, and then of the nurses in the military hospital back home. He'd flirted wickedly with those nurses, making a joke of the humiliation of being helpless.

He couldn't have flirted to save his life when Ellie had been struggling with that zipper. He'd been looking down at her bent head. The rope of black hair was still dripping wet, but the fronds that the wind had whipped free were starting to dry and they were softening the outlines of her face. Or they would have been if it wasn't set in such grim lines of determination.

She *really* didn't want to be touching him, did she? This

was an ordeal she was forcing herself to get through because she had no choice.

Like being unrecognised, this was an alien experience for a man almost bored by the way women threw themselves at him. Not a pleasant experience either, but it wasn't humiliation or even embarrassment that was so overwhelming. He couldn't begin to identify *what* it was he was feeling. He just knew that it was powerful enough to be disturbing.

Very disturbing.

The choice of trousers *was* embarrassing with the only pair he had any hope of fitting being shapeless track pants that didn't cover his ankles. At least the socks looked long and he could be grateful there were no paparazzi around.

'What will we do with the wet gear?'

Ellie had taken the lamp down from the hook on the ceiling and was pouring something from a plastic bottle into its base.

'We'll hang them over the chairs. They might be dry enough to get back into by the time we get rescued from here.'

'How long do you reckon that'll be?'

Ellie had the glass cover off the lamp now. She struck a match and held it to a wick. 'We had a lot of info coming in about the cyclone while we were in the air. The worst of it won't hit until early tomorrow, but it should blow through within about twelve hours.'

The flame caught and Ellie eased the glass cover back into place. She fiddled with an attachment to the base, pumping it gently, and suddenly the light increased to a glow that seemed like a spotlight focused on her. As she looked up and caught his gaze, a hint of a smile made her lips curve. 'It's going to get worse before it gets better, I'm afraid.'

Jake's mouth felt suddenly dry.

Even the hint of a smile transformed Ellie's face. Made it come alive.

She was an extraordinarily beautiful woman. He could actually feel something slamming shut in his chest. Or his head maybe.

*Don't go there. Don't get sucked in. Even if she doesn't know who you are, it's not worth the risk.*

*Remember what happened last time.*

But Ellie stretched to hang the lamp from its hook and the unbuttoned sleeves of her oversize shirt fell back to expose slim, olive-brown arms. Long, clever fingers made another adjustment to the base of the lamp.

Jake couldn't drag his gaze free.

Yeah…it probably *was* going to get worse before it got better.

But he could deal with it.

He *had* to.

# CHAPTER FOUR

THE KEROSENE LAMP hissed and swayed gently in the draughts that were a soft echo of the fierce storm outside. The glow of light strengthened as day became night and shadows danced in the corners of the room as the light moved—a dark partner to the bright flicker of the flames in the open fireplace.

The room was warm enough for the wet clothing draped over the spindle-back chairs to be steaming gently and one end of the table was covered with a collection of items that had come from the pockets of Ellie's flight suit, like a bunch of keys, ruined ballpoint pens and an equally wet and useless mobile phone. Most importantly, there was a two-way radio that had been securely enclosed in a waterproof pouch.

Jake had been disappointed that they couldn't use it to listen and hear updates on the weather, but Ellie was more concerned about whether it was in working order. It didn't seem to be transmitting.

'Medic One to base—do you receive?'

A crackle of static and a beeping noise came from the device, but there was no answering voice. Ellie gave up after a few tries.

'We may be out of range or it could be atmospheric conditions. I'll turn it on in the morning and we might get communication about our rescue.'

The radio sat on the edge of the table now—a symbol of surviving this ordeal.

Except, for the moment, it didn't seem to be that much of an ordeal. They were safe and finally warm. And Ellie had discovered a store of tinned food in the bottom of a cupboard.

'Chilli baked beans, cheesy spaghetti, Irish stew, peas or tomatoes.' She held up each can to show Jake. 'As my guest, you get to choose. What do you fancy?'

'They all sound good. I don't think I've ever been this hungry in my life.'

'Hmm…' Ellie had almost forgotten what it felt like to really smile. 'That's not a bad idea. I'll see if I've got a pot that's big enough.'

The result of mixing the contents of all the chosen cans together was remarkably tasty. Or maybe she was just as hungry as Jake. Whatever the reason, sitting cross-legged in front of the fire, spooning the food from a bowl, Ellie decided that it was probably one of the most memorable meals she would ever eat.

'There's more in the pot if you're still hungry,' she told Jake.

'Maybe we should save it for tomorrow.'

'There's still more cans. My mother must have stocked up big time on their last trip.'

'When was that?'

'Six years ago. I didn't come on that trip because I was in the middle of my helicopter training.' Ellie stared into the fire. 'Who knew it would save my life?'

'How d'you mean?'

'Their yacht ran into trouble on the way home. Both my parents drowned.'

'Oh…I'm sorry.'

Ellie could see Jake put his plate down suddenly, as if his appetite had deserted him. She kicked herself mentally.

'No, *I'm* sorry. I didn't mean to remind you of...' Her voice trailed into silence. He didn't want to talk about Ben, did he? She didn't need to glance sideways at his bent head to remind her of that walled-off private area. It was none of her business, anyway.

But she heard Jake take a deep breath a moment later. And then he shook his head as he got to his feet. He shoved his hair behind his ears.

'You wouldn't have a rubber band or a piece of string or something, would you? My hair's going to drive me nuts if I don't tie it back.'

Ellie blinked. 'I can find something.' She couldn't help a personal question. 'Why do you wear it so long if it annoys you?'

'Not my choice. It's temporary. You could say it's a—a work thing.'

'Ohh...' Ellie was bemused. 'What are you—a male model?'

Jake's breath came out in a snort. 'Something like that.'

Ellie could well believe it. She'd seen that body. The dark wavy hair that almost brushed his shoulders would probably be wildly exciting for a lot of women, too, but the beard? No...it wouldn't do it for her.

She almost changed her mind as Jake used his fingers to rake his hair back properly from his face. Even with the beard hiding half his face, she had trouble dragging her gaze away from him.

'What? Have I got spaghetti on my face or something?'

'No...you just look...I don't know...different.'

Different but oddly familiar. Or was that simply a warning signal that something unconscious was recognising the magnetic pull this man seemed to have? Ellie turned away with a decisive enough head movement to make her aware of the heavy weight of her own hair. The loose bits had long since dried, but the braid was still wet.

'Here. Have this…' She pulled the elastic band from the end of her braid. 'I need to get my hair dry and it'll take all night if I leave it tied up.'

So Jake bound his hair back in a ponytail and Ellie unravelled hers and let it fall over her back with the ends brushing the wooden boards of the floor. Now it was Jake's turn to stare, apparently. She could feel the intensity of his gaze from where he was sitting on the sofa behind her.

Was it the hissing of the lamp or the crackle of the fire or was there some kind of other current in the air that Ellie could actually *feel* instead of hear? It had all the intensity of a bright light and the heat of a flame and something warned Ellie not to turn her head.

The current was coming from Jake.

She heard him clear his throat. As though he thought his speech might be hoarse if he didn't?

'Must have been tough, losing your parents like that. Have you got any brothers or sisters?'

'Nope.'

'Husband? Boyfriend? Significant other?'

'Nope.' Ellie felt her hackles rise. It was none of his business. He wasn't about to let her into personal areas. Why would he think she was willing to share?

'Sorry. Didn't mean to pry.' Jake's voice was flat. 'I just thought…it's going to be a long night and it might be kind of nice to get to know each other.'

Did that mean that if she was prepared to share, he might too? That she might even find out the significance of that intriguing tattoo, even?

'Fair enough.' But Ellie got to her feet. 'Let me find us some blankets and pillows first, if they're useable. And

I'll boil some water. We don't have milk, but there's probably a tin of cocoa or something around. We need a drink.'

It was some time before Ellie was satisfied they had all they needed for a while. The fire was well banked up with wood. They both had a blanket and a pillow and, by tacit consent, Jake would have the couch to try and sleep on while Ellie curled up in the armchair. Neither of them wanted to move any further away from the fire.

Exhaustion was taking over now. Her body ached all over and her injured ankle was throbbing badly despite the hastily applied strapping with a damp bandage that she'd found in one of her suit pockets when changing her clothes.

It had been one of the longest days of Ellie's life and the physical exertion had been draining enough without the added stress of the emotional side of it all. Not only the fear for her own safety but also the grief of knowing that the job was no longer enough to shield her from what she had run from.

Maybe part of it was renewed grief for the family she'd lost. Impossible for that not to be surfacing now that she'd finally come back to a place she'd been avoiding for that very reason.

And maybe that was what made her prepared to talk about it. About things she'd never had anyone to talk to about.

'I haven't been here since my parents died,' she told Jake. 'It was bad enough when we all came here after Grandpa died and I didn't want to come back knowing that I had no family left.' She sighed softly. 'I didn't have a boat anyway. I wasn't sure I wanted anything more to do with the sea.'

'Hard to get away from, I would think, when you live on an island.'

'Well—it's a big island, but you're right. The home I

grew up in is in Devonport in Auckland and it's right on the beach. I still live there. There's salt water in my family's blood, I reckon. That's why Grandpa took the job as the lighthouse-keeper on Half Moon Island.'

'The moon… Yeah, I heard you say something about that on the radio.'

'I recognised it from the air. I spent so much time there when I was little that it's like part of the family. That's a picture of it over there, on the wall.'

'I thought most lighthouses were automatic now.'

'They are. And Half Moon was automated long before I was born, but Grandpa couldn't bear to leave it behind. That's why he bought this patch of land and virtually lived here from when my dad was a teenager. I sailed up with them every school holiday until he died when I was seventeen. And then Mum, Dad and I still came at least a couple of times a year. Having Christmas here when all the pohutukawa trees are in full bloom is quite something. And we could still go over to Half Moon and explore. It's got an amazing amount of birdlife. It should be a national reserve.'

'Why isn't it?'

Ellie shrugged. 'Too remote, I guess. And it would be too expensive to run a pest eradication programme.'

She was so tired now, her eyes were drooping shut. That was enough of a foray into personal space, wasn't it?

Apparently not.

'I don't get it.' Jake's words broke a silence in which Ellie had been drifting closer to sleep.

'What?'

'Why someone like you is all alone.'

'Someone like me?' Ellie opened heavy lids and turned her head far enough to find Jake staring at her again.

'Yeah… Someone talented, incredibly brave…gorgeous…'

His words were doing something to her stomach. It felt like she'd swallowed one of the flames from the fireplace and it was tickling her with tendrils hot enough to be uncomfortable.

It made a response easy to find. 'Once burned, twice shy, you know?'

'Oh, I do know.' The words were laced with bitterness. 'What happened?'

'Same old story. Fell in love. Got betrayed. I won't bore you with the details, but it would have made a pretty good story line for a soap opera.'

The huff of sound that came from Jake managed to encompass both disgust and empathy. 'Good way to look at it, anyway.'

'How's that?'

'Like it's a movie and you can see the whole disaster up there on the big screen.'

A strangled sound of mirth escaped Ellie. 'And what would the humiliated, heartbroken heroine do in this movie?'

Jake's voice was soft. 'Pretty much what you've done. Got on with her life and turned herself into a real-life heroine.'

Ellie didn't want to hear any more of his praise. 'Life's not a movie,' she muttered.

'Helps to look at it like that sometimes, though.'

That woke Ellie up a little. Annoyed her, in fact. 'How does avoiding reality help exactly?'

'Because you see your life up on the screen and you're part of the audience. How would you feel if you were watching yourself giving up? Pulling the blankets over your head or crying in a corner? You wouldn't think it was worth watching any more, would you? Isn't it better to be cheering yourself on as you face the obstacles and overcome them?'

'Is that what you do?'

'Kind of, I suppose.' Ellie got the impression she was hearing something very personal here. 'Gets you through the tough bits.'

'The "fake it till you make it" school of thought?'

'Uh-uh.' The negative sound was very American. 'It's not fake. You're not pretending to be someone *else*. You're practising being the best person you can be, even if it feels like the skin doesn't quite fit yet.'

Had she annoyed him this time? The lapse into another silence suggested she had.

'So…' Ellie tried to keep her tone light. 'I'm guessing you're not married either?'

'Not anymore.'

It shouldn't make any difference to know he was single so why did her heart rate pick up a little?

'Used and abused, too, huh?'

'You said it.'

This time the silence felt like a door slamming. There was no point waiting for Jake to say anything else and his guard was up so firmly that Ellie wondered if she'd imagined that she'd been allowed briefly into a personal space. Instinct told her that if she pushed, that barrier would only get bigger.

She backed away. 'What's the happy ending going to be in the movie of my life, then? Do I get swept off my feet by the love of my life? Some gorgeous guy that I have no trouble trusting absolutely?'

'Of course.' There was a smile in Jake's voice that almost felt like praise. For not prying, perhaps?

She had to dismiss the fairy tale, though. 'That's why I don't watch movies. What's the point in escaping into fiction instead of facing reality?'

'If we couldn't hope for something better, life could be a pretty miserable business sometimes for a lot of folks.'

'I suppose.' Ellie snuggled deeper into her blanket and let her head sink into the pillow. 'Can't see it happening for me.'

'Me neither.'

The agreement felt like a connection. They were on the same page. And maybe what he'd said about playing a role had some merit. She could try faking it a bit herself.

'I'm happy with my reality,' she said. 'Why would I risk that happiness by hanging it on someone else? When it really boils down, the only person you can trust is yourself. Unless...' The words were sleepy now. Almost a murmur. 'Unless you've got a twin. That would be like having two of yourself.'

Jake said nothing and Ellie drifted closer to sleep, happy that they had got to know each other a little better. Had found a connection of sorts, albeit a negative one, in that relationships were currently a no-go area for both of them. Did that open the door, perhaps, to a friendship without the hidden agenda that always seemed to become a problem?

No. In those last moments before losing consciousness, Ellie's mind—and her body—insisted on remembering how it had felt to be so close to Jake's bare skin. To touch him. And just the thought of it meant she could still actually feel that sizzle that had been in the air when she'd felt him staring at her back.

There would be an agenda there all right, even if she didn't want it.

And it might not be just Jake's agenda.

It was a sudden change of temperature that woke Jake from a fitful, nightmare-plagued slumber. A slap of cold air on his face.

Sitting up to see over the back of the sofa, he found Ellie struggling to open the outside door.

'What's happened? What's *wrong?*'

'Nothing.' Ellie was wearing a heavy, oilskin coat. Her hair was still loose, but she had a woollen hat pulled down over her ears. 'I just need to go to the bathroom.'

'Are you crazy?' Now fully awake, Jake realised that all hell seemed to have broken out beyond the walls of their small shelter. The howling shriek of the wind was as unearthly as the weird half-light of the new day. Rain hammered at the tin roof and there was an ominous banging noise that suggested a piece of the roofing was coming loose.

Ignoring painfully stiff muscles and joints, he got to his feet and close to the window in time to see the meat safe give up any attempt to stay attached to the porch wall and the wind pick it up and send it bouncing into the trees.

'Wow...' Ellie sounded impressed by the force of the wind.

And she was planning to go out there? 'It's dangerous,' Jake growled.

'It's urgent,' Ellie said calmly. 'It's only a few steps. It's not as if I'm in danger of getting blown over a cliff or something.'

'There's branches flying everywhere. You could get hurt.' It was the sheer stupidity of what she was intending to do that was making Jake sound fierce. Or was it a sudden urge to protect this woman?

'You can get hurt crossing the road.'

She wasn't about to listen to him and who was he to tell her about assessing risk anyway? This woman dangled on thin wires underneath helicopters for a living, for goodness' sake.

'There's a pot of water on the stove,' Ellie told him. 'I'll be back by the time you've made us some cocoa.'

He could do that. He should do that instead of standing here by the window watching as Ellie bent almost double to force herself forward against the wind. It looked like she wasn't going to get the narrow door of the outhouse open against the wind, but he saw her wedge her boot inside a crack and then use her shoulder to force it open further.

Man...her strength was impressive, but her determination was downright intimidating.

Jake rubbed his eyes as he turned back to the stove. Not that he needed to be any more awake but there were still fragments of his nightmares that were swirling in his head.

Ellie—looking like a warrior princess with her long hair flowing in the wind behind her—pointing a finger at him and shouting.

*Fake...fake...fake...*

And Ben had been standing beside her. Equally accusing.

*Play-acting... Just like Mom... You can't face reality.*

But you're another me. I'm another you.

No. Jake prised the lid off the cocoa tin with the edge of a spoon. Ellie had been way off the mark with that sleepy observation. He and Ben had always been a unit, for sure—united against the outside world—but there were two distinct parts of that unit. They weren't the same person—not by a long shot.

Not even two halves of a whole. More like yin and yang. Very different but a perfect fit together.

And he'd never feel the same shape if Ben was gone.

But she hadn't been so far off the mark in suggesting that using a movie mode was sidestepping reality. Or Ben had been when he'd said pretty much the same thing in the life raft. Wasn't that pretty much how it had all started, even though he'd been far too young to realise what he was doing?

The water in the pot was boiling now. Ellie had been gone quite long enough so any second now she would burst back in through the door. Jake tipped water into the mugs, grateful for the need to focus and the distraction of the rich smell of chocolate. He could get on with surviving another day and banish the last of those disturbing dreams.

Especially the one where he hadn't been able to tell himself apart from his brother. When it was him who was lost on that unforgiving ocean. Tossed out of the life raft and dragged deeper and deeper under the weight of icy water. *Drowning...*

The explosive cracking noise from outside was more than enough to send that dream fragment into oblivion. It was enough to drain the blood from Jake's face. The whole house seemed to be shaking and the noise just got louder. One of the mugs toppled over and steaming liquid poured onto the floor, but Jake didn't notice. The light was changing. Getting darker. And then there was an impact that had all the force of an earthquake. The second mug crashed to the floor and shattered. A chair toppled. The kerosene lamp swung so violently the flame was extinguished.

The sound of any wind or rain felt like silence after that.

A very ominous silence.

Jake was already at the door, wrenching it open. He'd never shouted so loudly in his life.

*'Ellie...'*

## CHAPTER FIVE

SHE FELT THE first shudders of the ground just as she tried to open the door of the outhouse again.

She heard the terrible cracking that could only mean one thing. A tree was coming down. A very large tree.

Was she about to get crushed? Trapped in what was little more than a wooden box?

This was more terrifying than being dragged through that wave like a fish on a line yesterday. At least she'd had a crew looking out for her and elements of the situation she could control herself. As she felt the outhouse being picked up with her still inside it and thrown through the air, Ellie was convinced she was about to die.

Did she imagine hearing someone calling her name?

A split second of sheer longing overwhelmed her. She wanted to be inside the beach house. With Jake's arms around her. Holding her tight. Keeping her safe.

The impact of hitting the ground shattered the old wooden boards around her, but instead of seeing daylight, Ellie found she was inside a layer of branches and the stiff leaves of a pohutukawa tree. A layer so thick it was hard to breathe. Miraculously, she didn't seem to be injured. Curling onto her knees, she started snapping small branches around her face and pushing them away to clear a space.

*'Ellie...'*

She definitely hadn't imagined it this time.

'I'm here, Jake.'

'I can't see you.'

'I'm under branches. I… *Ahh*…' Ellie groaned with the effort of trying to snap a bigger branch.

'Oh, God…are you *hurt?*'

The concern in his voice was enough to bring a lump to Ellie's throat. She might not have the backing of an experienced rescue team right now, but there *was* someone there who seemed to care whether or not she was okay.

She had to swallow hard before she could shout back. 'I don't think so. I'm just…stuck.'

'I'll get you out. Keep shouting so I know where you are.'

Ellie did keep shouting. She kept trying to find a way through herself, too, squeezing herself through smaller gaps and turning away from branches so big they would need a chainsaw to break them. She could hear the snapping of wood as Jake tried to create a path from the other side of the massive tree canopy.

It was dirty work and exhausting and Ellie could feel the scratches and bruises she was accumulating on her bare face and hands. Her hair kept getting caught and having to be painfully wrenched free. She was going to get it cut off when she got out of here, she decided.

*If* she got out of here.

The next desperate attempt to wriggle through a gap was badly judged. Ellie's leg got caught and trying to get free only wedged her foot further into a fork of thick branches. It was her injured foot that was caught, too, and even trying to pull it clear brought a sob of both frustration and pain from deep in her chest.

'I *knew* you were hurt.' After what had seemed an interminable amount of time, there was Jake's face only inches from her own. 'How bad is it?'

'It's just my ankle. From yesterday. But…it's wedged… I can't…'

'I can.' Jake crawled further into the mess of tangled tree and took hold of her foot. 'Sorry—this might hurt a bit.' He held onto her ankle and eased it out of the boot with a seesawing motion. Without her foot inside, it was easy enough to pull the boot free.

And then he was showing her which way to crawl after him.

'We'll go around the roots. The path's not so blocked that way.'

It was so wrong, seeing the massive trunk horizontal to the ground, with half the roots snapped off and taller than Jake's head. He had his arm around Ellie, taking most of her weight as he helped her move forward against wind that felt like a wall that kept shoving them viciously, but Ellie's cry, as they stumbled on the uneven, disrupted earth that had been beneath the tree, halted their progress. They were on the edge of a large hole and the earth was crumbling.

'I'll carry you.'

'No—it's not that. *Look*…' She had to shout to make herself heard. This was worse than it had been on the beach but not simply because of the weather.

Jake pulled strands of hair away from his eyes as he turned his head to where she was pointing.

'What *is* it? A rat?'

'It's a kiwi. A brown kiwi.' He wasn't to know how rare and precious this native bird was, but Ellie was too close to tears.

'Nothing we can do. It's been squashed. We've got to get inside or it'll be us next.'

But Ellie shook her head. 'There might be a nest. We've got to check.'

Jake was looking at her as if she was crazy. Could he see the tears that were now escaping? How important this was to her?

He stared at her for just a heartbeat longer. 'You stay here. What am I looking for?'

'A burrow. An egg…or a baby…'

Jake slipped as he stepped down into the hole and there he was on his hands and knees, with a cyclone raging around them, looking to rescue a small creature that could be in danger because it was important to Ellie.

He didn't even know what a kiwi was, so it couldn't matter to him.

He was doing this for *her*.

A piece of her heart felt like it was breaking away. Ready to offer to Jake? And then he was coming back— streaked with dirt and a trickle of blood on his forehead— with a huge, creamy egg in his hands. The wind was even louder now and Jake didn't bother trying to say anything.

He put the egg inside the boot that had come off El- lie's foot, shoved it into her hands and then kept one arm firmly around her body as he pulled them forward for the short distance back to the house.

'Let me look at that ankle.'

'No. I have to look at the egg first.'

What was it with this egg?

Okay, he'd heard of kiwis. It was what New Zealand- ers called themselves, wasn't it? Weird enough that they identified so strongly with some flightless bird, but was it that big a deal?

Had he really kept them both out there in such dangerous conditions because she was so worried that there might be an orphaned chick or egg?

Yeah… But he'd seen the tears, hadn't he? And coming from the bravest woman he'd ever met, they had been shocking.

Now the whole episode felt ridiculous. Jake ignored Ellie as she eased the egg out of the boot and examined it. He picked up a toppled chair and unhooked the lamp so that she could show him how to light it again. As the room brightened, however, her exclamation made him stop and join her at the table.

'Look at this.'

It was a hole at one end of the egg. Something was poking out of it.

'Must have got damaged when the tree came down. Shame.' Was Ellie going to start crying again and, if so, what would he do about it this time? Hold her in his arms?

But she was smiling. 'It's called an external pip. It's *hatching*.'

'No way…'

Even more astonishing was the way Ellie picked up the egg and sniffed at the hole.

'What *are* you doing?'

'I want to know how far along it is. Sometimes you can tell by the smell whether the chick's all sweaty and in trouble.'

'How on earth do you know that?'

'My granddad was passionate about birds. We looked after a lot of them on the island. And I volunteer, these days, at a captive rearing centre that's trying to save endangered kiwi. It's run by one of my best friends, Jillian. We look after eggs and chicks and then release them back into the wild.'

Okay. It was official now. Eleanor Sutton was the most

extraordinary woman Jake had ever met. He knew he was staring and probably looking vaguely starstruck.

Ellie simply shrugged. 'I've got a thing for nature, that's all. Enough Maori blood in me to revere the land. And our *taonga*. The treasure.'

Something fell into place. That gorgeous, olive skin and the impressive mane of black hair. The fighting spirit. It wasn't surprising in the least that Ellie was in some part descended from a warrior race.

But he had to stop staring at her so he stared at the egg instead. 'How long does it take to hatch?'

'Can be days but there's no way of knowing how long it's been already... Oh, look...'

The bump that had been protruding from the egg suddenly got longer. A piece of shell broke free and then he could see the head attached to the strange-looking beak. A tiny eye amongst wet-looking feathers.

In fascinated silence, they both perched on the edge of the spindle-backed chairs and watched as the chick struggled free.

It took a while and every so often they both raised their heads to make eye contact with each other. They were both witnesses to what seemed like a small miracle in the face of such destruction going on in the outside world. The shriek of the wind and the sound of the driving rain on the tin roof punctuated by the occasional bang of a branch hitting it was no more than a background at the moment. They were sharing the birth of something new and amazing.

Jake knew that whatever else happened in his life he would remember this. Ellie and the kiwi chick. New life. This was important. Momentous, even.

It was the strangest baby bird Jake had ever seen—totally out of proportion with a small head, long beak, distended belly and huge feet.

But Ellie was rapt. Her eyes were glowing. 'Congratulations, Dad.'

Jake snorted. If he'd felt ridiculous risking his life to save an egg, it was nothing compared to feeling parental pride over its hatching. And if he was the surrogate father, that made Ellie the mother. An almost wife scenario.

He glared at Ellie and she looked away quickly.

'We need to let it rest for fifteen minutes or so and then I can pick off any bits of shell and stuff. Then we need to keep it warm.'

'We need to check your ankle. And your face is a mess.'

Ellie's eyes widened, but she reached up and touched her face and then looked at her blood-streaked fingers.

'Soon. I need...' She twisted to look at what was draped over the back of the chair she was sitting on. 'Can you spare your thermal?'

'Sure.'

Ellie twisted the dry garment into a thick rope and then curled it into a circle, leaving a hollow in the centre. Very gently, she picked up the baby kiwi and placed it carefully into the hollow.

'They have a distended abdomen because of internalised yolk. It needs support so that it doesn't end up with splayed legs.' With a touch on the tip of its beak, so light it was no more than a thought, Ellie smiled. 'It needs a name, too.'

'I don't do baby names.' Jake turned away. 'I'll heat up some water so you can wash those scratches.'

'Pēpe,' he heard Ellie say softly behind him. 'It's Maori for baby.'

With Pēpe safely on his doughnut nest inside an old plastic container and close enough to the fire to keep warm, Ellie finally hobbled to the couch to check out the extent of her own injuries. Not that it mattered how bad her ankle felt or how awful her face must look. The miracle of the egg not only being viable but hatching was enough to make this whole ordeal worthwhile.

Her ankle certainly looked impressive, though. Her foot was so swollen her toes looked ridiculously small and the bruising down her ankle and along the sides of her foot was black and purple now.

Jake was horrified. Kneeling beside the sofa, he reached out to touch her foot.

'How bad does it feel?'

Ellie simply shrugged because right then she wasn't aware of any pain. All she could focus on was the feel of Jake's hands on her skin and how gentle they were as he traced the swelling and touched the tips of her toes.

'Can you feel that?'

Oh, yeah…

'Mmm. I've still got circulation.'

'Can you wriggle your toes?'

Yes. Ellie could.

'Can you press down against my hand?' He was cradling her foot on his fingers now.

Ellie actually grinned. 'Yes, Doctor. Oh… *Ouch.*' But she was still smiling. 'I'm sure it's only a sprain. I just need to strap it up again and rest it for a bit.'

'I'll strap it up.' Jake was rolling the dirty bandage he had helped her remove. 'Don't suppose you've got a dry one of these somewhere?'

'Hang it by the fire for a while. I won't try and walk until I've got my ankle wrapped up again.'

'I'll get the water. You can wash those scratches.'

Ellie nodded, but she was finally noticing how scratched Jake was himself, especially his hands. How hard had he worked to rescue her? And then she'd made him do more by sending him under the tree roots to look for the dead kiwi's nest.

How magic had it been, seeing the wonder of the chick hatching reflected in Jake's eyes every time she'd been able to look away from what they'd been watching?

And how gentle had he been in checking out her injuries?

Not that she was ready to put her trust in a man, but imagine if you *could* trust someone like Jake? So strong. Protective. Caring. Gentle…

So incredibly *male*…

She reached out to touch his arm as he got to his feet. 'I…I couldn't have got out of there by myself. And Pēpe would have died. Thank you…'

Was it intentional, the way he kept moving…escaping her touch? He looked down at her again and his mouth was twisted into a crooked smile.

A very endearing smile.

'Guess that makes us even, then,' he said gruffly. 'Equal partners?'

'Yeah…' Ellie was still caught by that smile. By the intensity of those dark eyes. Beneath all that hair, Jake Logan was an extraordinarily good-looking man.

He looked away first. 'So maybe next time you'll listen to me when I say something's dangerous.'

'Maybe…'

Outside, the storm still raged, but Ellie felt safe again.

More than safe. She felt cared for. By someone who had as much to give as she did. An ideal partner. There weren't many men who could match Ellie Sutton in terms of courage and resourcefulness. They had a lot in common, didn't they? Not only a spirit of adventure and the fortitude to deal with adversity but they'd both been burned by love. Not that Jake had shared any personal details about the marriage that didn't exist any longer, but that didn't break a sense of connection that only strengthened as the long day wore on.

Frequent checking of the baby bird created a shared pleasure that he seemed to be doing well.

'He's so fluffy now that he's dry,' Jake commented, crouched beside the container and staring into it intently.

'They're unusual feathers,' Ellie told him. 'Kiwis don't need to fly so they're more for warmth. More like hair than feathers.'

'How long until he can go back to the wild?'

'I'll take him to the centre back in Auckland. Jillian will want to put him in a brooder unit for a few weeks and, if he's healthy enough, he'll only need a few more weeks in a quarantine period. They can put a transponder on him and hopefully I can bring him back here. Or, even better, I might be able to release him on Half Moon Island. Grandpa would have been thrilled by that.'

'I'd love to see that. If I'm still in the country.'

Ellie wasn't sure how to respond to that. Give him her phone number? Ask him for his? Admit that she'd be keen to see him again? The ramifications were alarming.

'I'll have to see if it's even possible,' she said cautiously. 'There's lots of regulations.'

'Of course.'

Jake's expert bandaging of her ankle was something else that bound them into more of a team.

'I couldn't have done that better myself. You're not actually a doctor, are you? Or a medic?'

'I've learned a bit of first aid in my time. What with the army and stuff.'

So she'd been right. The limp was probably a legacy of being a soldier.

'Afghanistan?'

'Yep. A long time ago.'

And his tone told her that he still didn't want to talk about anything personal. Ellie got that. What was harder to get her head around was the intense curiosity she was developing. She had so many questions she wanted to ask. So much she wanted to know about this man. And it was more than mere curiosity, if she was honest with herself. This felt more like longing.

A longing to let go?

To trust again?

Maybe he wouldn't have to warn her about something dangerous.

Perhaps he *was* that something.

They slept for a while in the afternoon and by the time they woke it was obvious that the storm had eased considerably. There wasn't much daylight left, though, so perhaps they would be here for another night.

Ellie eased her legs off the couch as Jake stood up. They needed some more firewood if they had a second night to get through and it was past time to check on Pēpe again. Her first attempt to get to her feet failed, however, and she sat back down with a rush.

'Here...' Jake offered her a hand. 'Take it easy, though. That foot won't want much weight on it.'

He held out his other hand as Ellie started to rise and, a heartbeat later, she found herself on her feet, holding both Jake's hands.

And he wasn't letting go.

Ellie certainly couldn't let go first. For one thing her hands were encased by his and for another her body simply wouldn't cooperate. She couldn't even look away from his face. From a gaze that was holding hers with a look that made the rest the world cease to exist. Everything seemed

to coalesce. Surviving the rescue, finding their way to shelter, being rescued herself and the bond that had grown and
grown today, thanks to Jake's heroism in saving the egg.
So many, powerful emotions.

His face was so close. She only had to lean a little and
tilt her face up and her lips would meet his.

And, dear Lord…she could feel it happening and no
alarm bells were going to halt the process, no matter how
loudly they tried to sound.

She was so close now she could feel his breath on her
lips and her eyes were drifting shut in anticipation of a
kiss she wanted more than anything she could remember
wanting in her life.

The sharp crackle of static from behind made her jump.

'Medic One, do you read? Ellie…are you there?'

# CHAPTER SIX

A MOMENT HAD never been broken so decisively.

Jake froze. Ellie dived for the radio.

'Medic One receiving. Mike, is that you?'

Another crackle of static and Ellie's heart sank. Maybe she could receive but not transmit.

'...on our way. Can you...on the beach in twenty...?'

Ellie was used to filling in gaps in broken messages. *'Yes.'* Radio protocol was forgotten. 'We'll be there.' Aware of the intense focus of Jake, who was still standing as still as a stone, Ellie pushed the transmitting button again and held it down. 'Mike? Any news on...on the other man in the life raft?'

She held her breath through another burst of static. What if there was no news or—worse—bad news? Jake would be devastated and she would be the one who'd been the bearer of the news. He might shoot the messenger and she would never get as close to him again as she had a moment ago.

A curious wash of something like grief came from no-where. Ellie could actually feel the sting of tears behind her eyes.

'...fine...' The unexpected word burst through the static. 'Washed onto island...taken to... Be in Auckland by the time you... Ellie, have you any idea who...?'

It didn't matter that the rest of the message was lost. Or

that Ellie still had tears in her eyes as she turned to Jake. He wouldn't notice anyway. She could see that he was shaking and he had a hand shielding his eyes as though he didn't want anyone to see whatever overwhelming emotion he was experiencing.

If she went to him and put her arms around him he would probably kiss her, Ellie realised. But would it be only because he needed an outlet for the joyous relief he was struggling to control?

But when he dropped his hand, his face looked haggard. 'I can't believe it,' he said hoarsely. 'I *won't* believe it…not until I see Ben again.'

'Let's move, then.' The switch of professionalism was easy to flick. Could still provide protection, even. Ellie didn't have time to indulge in any personal reactions. 'We need to change our clothes, put the fire out and get ourselves—and Pēpe—down to the beach. There's not enough daylight left to muck the crew around.'

The media were waiting.

No surprises there. It was enough of a story to have an elite yacht race decimated by the worst storm in decades and they had probably been earning their keep for the last couple of days editing and broadcasting film of dramatic rescues, interviews with survivors and heart-wrenching intrusions on the families of those killed or missing.

What a bonus to have an A-list celebrity as one of the survivors. The paparazzi would be fighting for the best spot to get a photograph that would earn big money. Any one of his favoured charities could be in for an enormous windfall when he chose the best offer for magazine coverage. And not only was Jake a survivor, there was a juicy glimpse into his family life thrown in. Coverage of the twin brother who'd successfully evaded any media spotlight until now because he hated the whole industry so much, thanks to what it had done to their mother. Their childhood.

The story would just keep growing legs, wouldn't it? A savvy journalist could delve into their background and rake over their father's reputation as an utterly ruthless businessman. Their mother's degeneration into reliance on prescription medication and alcohol, which had been her ultimate downfall.

Or had it?

He had to get to Ben. To talk to him.

The shouting from the gathered crowd as the helicopter landed took over from the noise of the slowing rotors as the doors were opened.

'Jake…'

'Mr Logan… This way…'

'Dr Jon… Code One…'

Good grief. Did someone think he would respond to the name of a character he played instead of his real name? It wasn't so stupid, though, was it? He almost turned towards the incessant flash of camera lights in that direction. Instead, he looked back to where Ellie was being helped from the helicopter. She was still clutching the container that held the baby kiwi and seemed to be arguing with her colleague over whether she was fit to walk on that ankle. Jake felt his lips twitching and suppressed a smile. Good luck to someone who wanted to make Ellie do something she didn't want to do.

But then she looked up and saw the media. She had to be hearing all the yelling of his name. She really hadn't had any idea of who he was, had she? No wonder she was looking so bewildered. The man beside her was grinning. He raised an arm to wave at the photographers and television crews. And then he was saying something to Ellie and she turned her head to stare at *him*.

She looked horrified.

Betrayed, even.

There was nothing he could do about it. People from his film production crew were here, too. The director and his PR manager were coming towards him and there was a black limousine with tinted windows waiting with its doors open on this side of the fence that was keeping the media at a respectable distance. An ambulance, with its back doors also open, was parked near the limousine.

'Jake… *Mate*…I can't tell you how good it is to see you. Let's get you to hospital for a check-up.'

'Don't need it,' Jake said.

'We do,' the director insisted. 'Insurance protocol.'

'Do you know where my brother is?'

'No. We do know he's okay, though. You can see him as soon as you've been given the all-clear.'

Ellie and her fellow paramedic were close now. The man had his arm around Ellie, supporting her as she limped. He couldn't hold her gaze. She seemed to lean into her companion, looking up as he spoke to them.

'Survivors have all been taken to The Cloud. Big building down at the Viaduct on the waterfront,' he told Jake. 'There's a medical team there and it's not far from the hospital if they decide you need attention. That's where we're taking Ellie—to the hospital.'

He kept moving, steering Ellie towards the ambulance. For a crazy moment Jake almost followed them—just to stay close to Ellie for a little longer. Who knew when or even if they would ever see each other again? He wanted…

He didn't know what he wanted. To try and explain why he hadn't told her who he was? To try and figure out if this guy she worked with was more than a colleague?

No. He did know what he wanted. What he had to do first.

'Take me to this cloud building,' he ordered his director. 'I'll do whatever I have to but not until I've seen Ben.'

'The media will be all over you.'

'I'll cope.'

'We've got a film crew tailing us.' Mike peered through the small windows at the back of the ambulance. 'You're famous, El.'

'I was just doing my job.' Ellie sat back on the stretcher, letting her head rest on the pillows. She closed her eyes, her breath escaping in a ragged sigh. 'I hope Dave's being careful, taking Pēpe to the centre.'

'He will be. He loves a challenge that's a bit different. You want some pain relief?'

'No. I'm fine.' Apart from feeling gutted without having any reasonable grounds.

The only sound for a moment was the rumble of the truck's engine.

'Did you really have no idea who he was?'

Her eyes snapped open. 'How could I? He didn't *tell* me.'

'Not even his name?'

'Well…yeah. He told me his name. It was just a name.'

Mike snorted. 'You've just spent more than twenty-four hours holed up with one of the most eligible males in the universe. Most girls would kill for an opportunity like that.

It was Ellie's turn to snort.

'*ER* used to be your favourite TV show. You must remember that French surgeon. What was his name? Pierre or something. And then the *Stitch in Time* series? Where that modern doctor keeps going through that portal and saving lives that change the course of history?'

Ellie shook her head. She hadn't seen it. And it had been

years since *ER* had been her entertainment fix. Jake would have been ten years younger and wouldn't have been disguised by far too much hair. She never knew the real names of actors anyway—she had enough trouble remembering the names of the characters they portrayed. But it made a horrible kind of sense.

No wonder Jake could act like a doctor. Gentle and caring and skillful. He'd learned how to pretend to *be* one, hadn't he?

'That's what he was coming to New Zealand for. To film the last bits of the movie they're making from the series. You wouldn't believe the coverage the E channel's been giving this disaster thanks to him being in it. And did you know that the other guy in the life raft was his brother? Not just a brother but his *twin?*'

'Yes. I did know that.'

Everybody would know that. Was that why Jake had revealed that much? And was the reason he'd been so shuttered about anything else personal because he knew it would be gold for the waiting media and he didn't trust her not to go and spill the beans?

The television crew had beaten the ambulance to the hospital. They were waiting for Ellie to come out of the back. A couple of photographers were there as well.

'Ms Sutton…how are you feeling?'

'What can you tell us about Jake Logan? Is he coming here as well?'

'You saved his life… How does he feel about that?'

'Ellie—over here. Slow down… We just need one shot.'

Ellie ducked her head behind Mike's arm. 'For heaven's sake,' she muttered. 'Just get me inside.'

The Cloud was an extraordinary building right on the waterfront of Auckland's harbour. Designed to accommodate up to five thousand people, it was long and low with an undulating white roof that had given it the unusual name. A perfect space to be catering for the huge numbers of people.

The Ultraswift-Round-the-World yacht race had come to a temporary halt due to Cyclone Lila. The boats that had made it safely to Auckland were all moored nearby and their crews were using The Cloud as their base as they had repairs done on their yachts and waited for the weather to settle. Families of those injured or still missing were here as well, and there were almost as many reporters as the race officials, crews and their supporters.

Jake was hustled through the crowd and allowed to ignore the press of attention. He was taken to a mezzanine level at the far end of the building that had been roped off to allow only authorised personnel. Up the stairs and in a private area of a large bar, Ben was waiting.

He had apparently refused to allow their reunion to be anything other than completely private and, as the two men held each other in a grip powerful enough to prevent a breath being taken and Jake felt the trickle of tears on his face, he had never been more thankful that the moment wasn't going to be shared with the world.

It was a long time before they broke apart enough to stare intently at each other.

'I thought I'd lost you.'

'Me, too.'

'I couldn't believe it. I *didn't* believe it until now. Are you okay?'

'Pretty good. Got a bit banged up and dislocated my knee. I'll be on crutches for a week or two. And I wouldn't mind sitting down again.'

There were comfortable chairs here. A small table had been provided with a cushion on it for Ben to keep his leg supported. A pair of elbow crutches lay on the floor be-side the table. Apart from the splint on his knee, though, Ben didn't seem to have suffered a major injury.

'How did you do it? What happened after I got rescued? It felt like the worst moment in my life when I found out that the weather had got so bad they couldn't even *try* to get back to rescue you.'

Ben looked about as haggard as Jake was feeling. He was nodding and it looked as if he was swallowing hard before he could answer. 'And the worst moment of mine was thinking I'd never see you again.'

'So what happened?'

'Bit of a blur. Didn't think I was going to make it. Thought I was dead until I found myself being dragged up a beach.'

'Someone *found* you?'

'Wouldn't be here if they hadn't. And it wasn't just someone. It was a nurse who goes by the name of Smash 'em Mary.'

Jake had to grin. 'Sounds formidable.'

Something flickered in Ben's eyes but was gone before Jake could analyse it. 'She saved my life,' was all he said. 'And she was a nurse. If she hadn't put my knee back I'd be a lot worse off than I am now.'

'You got saved by a nurse.' Jake shook his head. 'And I got saved by a paramedic. A *girl* paramedic.'

Except that 'girl' was totally the wrong word. Coura-geous, determined...beautiful...Eleanor Sutton was a pow-erful woman. Compelling. And Jake was already...*missing* her? Not that he could begin to explain to Ben what had happened in the hours they'd been apart. It would have to wait until they had more time. Until Jake had had a chance to get his own head around what may well have been a life-changing incident. Best to ignore it for the moment.

'What happens now?'

'Guess I'll get the first flight I can back to the States. You?'

'I'll get on with what I was coming here for in the first place. There's a deadline on getting this film into the can.'

Ben nodded. 'We both need to get back into it. Put this disaster behind us.'

'Any word on *Rita*?'

'Doubt they'll even find any wreckage. She's gone.'

Just like her namesake. Rita Marlene. Their mother.

Jake closed his eyes and took a deep breath. 'What you said, Ben…it's not true. Mom didn't kill herself. It was an accident. That was the coroner's verdict.'

Ben was silent.

'It's *not* true,' Jake insisted. '*Is* it?'

'I wouldn't have said it if it wasn't true.'

'How do you know? Did you hide something? Like a *note?*'

Ben shook his head.

'So how do you know?' Jake's voice rose. 'You have to tell me. I've got a right to know.'

'I can't.'

'Can't…or *won't?*'

'Jake…' Ben held up his hands—a pleading gesture. 'Let it go. Please. It's so long ago it doesn't make any difference now.'

'Are you *kidding?* You can't say something like that and just leave it. If you've got some evidence and you've been hiding it all these years, you've been *lying* to me.'

'I haven't got any evidence. I just…*know.*'

'Jake?' It was his PR manager, Kirsty, who approached the men in their corner of this big space. 'Sorry to break in on the family reunion but we've got all the major TV networks queued up downstairs to talk to you. Adam's getting an ulcer, waiting for you to get a proper medical clearance. How long do you think you'll be?'

Jake glared at Ben. The joy of seeing his brother safe was being undermined by anger at not getting the answers he needed.

And there was fear there, too. Ben was the only person in the world he'd ever had complete faith in. Absolute trust.

He was looking completely shattered now. Instead of celebrating their joint survival, Jake had turned it into a confrontation that was something he'd never anticipated between them. Was he even ready to hear the truth?

And now they were being interrupted by the lifestyle that Ben deplored. The pursuit of fame that had always seemed more important to their mother than they had been. Play-acting. Sidestepping reality.

He could hear an echo of Ellie's voice in his head.

*How does avoiding reality help exactly?*

Maybe it didn't help but it was the only protection Jake knew.

Ben seemed to sense his train of thought. The softening in his eyes suggested that he understood. He gripped his brother's shoulder.

'Go, Jake. It's what you do. Your public needs you. *You* need them. We'll talk soon.' He even summoned a cheeky grin. 'And, hey…no amount of money could buy this kind of PR for the movie. You may as well milk it.'

'Amen,' said Kirsty. 'Come on, Jake. Pretty please… We'll set up a press conference so you only have to do it once. And while we're doing that, you can let the doctors check you out properly.'

X-rays had revealed no broken bones, but the ligament damage to Ellie's ankle meant that she needed a plaster cast for a couple of weeks at least. And complete rest. She was off active duty on the helicopter crew for the foreseeable future.

'I'm going to be bored out of my skull,' Ellie informed Mike, who had come back to hear the verdict and take her home.

'They'll find some light duties for you on base for a while.'

'Mmm.' Maybe fate was stepping in here, forcing her to take some time out and think about her future. Did she really want to give up on the part of her career that had meant so much to her for so long?

Right now, all Ellie wanted to do was to get home and eat something that hadn't come out of an ancient can. To call Jillian at the bird centre and get more information than Dave had passed on to Mike about the condition of the rescued baby kiwi. To sink into her own bed and sleep. A week or so should do the trick.

There was a slight problem with the plan, however.

'Where's my other boot?'

'You can't wear it with your foot in a cast.'

'No, but it had all the loose stuff from my pockets in it. I had to find a way to carry it all in a bit of a rush. My keys are in there.'

'You can't drive either.'

'My house key is on the same ring.'

'Haven't you got a spare?'

Ellie was too tired to be reasonable. 'I want my boot.'

'I'll ring the base. It might still be in the chopper.'

He ended his phone call a short time later. 'Dave reckons it went with some other clothing—to The Cloud.'

Ellie sighed. There had been a bundle of clothing. Jake had changed out of the horrendous trackpants and put his jeans back on, but either he'd run out of time or had become attached to his black-and-red-checked shirt because he had only put his coat on top and bundled his other belongings under an arm.

'Fine. That's on the way home, if you don't mind a quick detour.'

Mike's face lit up. 'And get a chance to rub shoulders with the rich and famous again? See you become world famous as the woman who rescued Jake Logan? I don't mind at all.'

'There'll be no rubbing shoulders,' Ellie warned. 'We get my boot and get out. I'm not in any mood to get interviewed.'

She had no intention of talking to Jake if she could avoid it. The shock of learning who he really was had more than one aspect that was making her cringe.

She'd made a joke about his limp. Ordered him to make himself useful. And had she really dismissed his whole career by suggesting that he might be a male *model?*

He hadn't enlightened her, though, had he?

And you didn't have to lie outright to be dishonest. You could lie by omission.

Arriving at their destination wearing their bright red flight-suits and with Ellie hopping on crutches should have attracted attention, but instead they slipped in virtually unnoticed. Everybody was crowded around an area that had been set up with a long table in front of a big screen.

Images of yachts and rescue scenes were providing a backdrop to a press conference. Jake sat centre stage, flanked by the man who'd met him at the helipad and others who were wearing lanyards and looked like race officials. Just under the mezzanine level of the building, there were people leaning over the balcony to watch as well and Ellie noticed she wasn't the only person on crutches here.

Jake's voice was clear and loud, not only because of the

lapel mike he was wearing but due to the rapt silence of an audience that was hanging on every word.

'…we thought that was it. And then we saw the chopper with the crewman on the end of the winch. Or should I say crewwoman?' Jake's headshake was slow and incredulous. 'I can't speak highly enough of the courage and skill of the New Zealand helicopter rescue service. You guys should be very, very proud of yourselves.'

Mike nudged Ellie, but she was heading purposefully towards someone on the edge of the crowd at the very front. A woman with blond hair and high heels, who was holding a clipboard. She'd been at the helipad with the other people who'd been waiting to whisk Jake off in that ridiculous limousine. Maybe she'd know where her boot was.

'Oh…you must be Ellie.' The woman's smile was very wide. 'I'm Kirsty. This is great. Can we get a shot of you and Jake together after this interview? I understand it was you that rescued Jake? That it was *your* beach house you used as shelter? And did you guys really watch a kiwi hatching? That's so *awesome*…'

Someone from the floor was asking a question about whether the race organisers were at fault for not postponing this leg of the race. One of the officials started explaining the cyclone's erratic path. A video clip of a weather map was now playing on the big screen.

Ellie looked at Kirsty's perfect hair and makeup. She might have been able to brush out the tangled mess of her own hair at the hospital and rebraid it but it was still filthy. And while the scratches and bruises on her face had been well cleaned, she didn't have a scrap of any makeup on to soften the effect.

'No,' she told Kirsty firmly. 'I look like I've been dragged through a hedge backwards.' It wasn't far from the truth, was it? If Jake had told people about Pēpe, maybe he'd also told them about saving her life by getting her out from under that tree? Wouldn't the media love that—to find that a movie star had morphed into a real live hero? But it felt like something private was being exploited.

'And I'm exhausted,' she added. 'I just want to find my boot and get home.'

'I had it sent to the front reception desk. I didn't know that you'd be coming to collect it in person. Are you sure I can't change your mind about a photo? Or a quick interview? There's a lot of people here who are super-keen to talk to you.'

The need for officials to deflect blame for the disaster the yacht race had become was still going on. Not needing to answer any questions for the moment, Jake was looking around the room. Ellie watched, using it as an excuse to ignore Kirsty's request even though she knew that she had to be very obvious, standing here on the edge of the crowd, not far from the end of the long table. Wearing bright red.

She was prepared for him to notice her.

What she wasn't prepared for was the effect of the eye contact.

For just a heartbeat, he held her gaze. Clung to it as though seeing her again was a huge relief. As if he'd been afraid of never seeing her again?

For just that infinitesimal fraction of time it felt like that moment when Ellie had known they were going to kiss. That the connection was far too strong to resist.

But then it was gone. So fast she could believe she had imagined it.

And Jake was interrupting the race official.

'There's no point in trying to blame anyone,' he said smoothly. 'It happened. Yacht racing is a risky business. I'd like to take this opportunity to say how devastated we all are that lives have been lost. And how incredibly grateful both my brother and myself are for being rescued. There's one person in particular that I will be grateful to for the rest of my life.'

'Who's that?' someone yelled.

Jake was smiling now. He stretched out a hand. 'Paramedic Eleanor Sutton. My real life heroine.'

Kirsty beamed, stepping aside slightly to allow Ellie to be seen more clearly.

Ellie cringed as cameras swung in her direction.

'They want you to join them.' Kirsty sounded excited now. 'Do you need some help?'

'No.' The word came out through gritted teeth. Jake had caught her gaze again as he'd stretched out that hand as an invitation to share his fame.

She must have imagined that connection she'd felt because it certainly wasn't there this time. This was Jake Logan the movie star looking at her and he wasn't the man she had rescued or shared the miracle of watching new life emerge with.

Couldn't anyone else see that he was only showing what he wanted the world to see?

That that warm smile and the over-the-top praise wasn't *real?*

She didn't know this man.

And she didn't want to. She had personal experience of a man who could make others believe whatever he wanted. An experience she would never repeat, thank you very much.

With nothing more than a dismissive shake of her head for Kirsty's benefit, Ellie turned and started moving.

She had to get out of there.

# CHAPTER SEVEN

IN THE END, it was the rescue base manager, Gavin Smith, who gave the media at least some of what they wanted, providing details of the horrific day from the viewpoint of the emergency services and fielding some awkward questions from journalists.

'Is it normal practice to keep a victim on the end of a winch line like that? Isn't it incredibly dangerous?'

'The pros and cons of any emergency situation are something our crews are trained to weigh up. The chopper was already fully loaded. The only way to get the men out of the life raft was to try and transfer them to the closest land.'

'So why didn't they go back for Jacob Logan's brother?'

'Not only had weather conditions worsened, the condition of a patient on board was also critical. The risk to everybody involved was simply too great.'

'So they just got abandoned?'

'They weren't abandoned.' The base manager stayed perfectly calm. 'By a stroke of luck, the paramedic who was on the winch knew the area well. She knew that they could find shelter.'

'Why won't Eleanor Sutton talk to the media? Has she been told not to? What went on that needs to be kept so private?'

Gavin's bland expression made the question lose any

significance. 'As far as I'm concerned, there's nothing to tell. Our crew did their job under exceptionally trying circumstances. Successfully, I might add. If one of them chooses not to be in the public eye for doing that job, I'm more than happy to respect that. Perhaps you should too.'

It didn't appear that they were going to.

The phone had been ringing from the moment Ellie had got home. The offers to buy her story were starting to get ridiculous. Thousands of dollars turned into tens of thousands as the days passed and she continued to refuse an interview or photographs.

Maybe Jake had had good reason to keep so much personal information to himself. He wasn't to know that she was financially secure in a mortgage-free house she had inherited from her parents. Or that she'd been earning good money for years with no dependants to share it with. How many people would be tempted by an offer of such a windfall?

And wouldn't the gossip magazines love an account of what now seemed like a personal revelation about how Jake Logan saw movies as a means of coping with adverse life events?

About how he didn't see role-playing as being fake but as a chance to practise being the best version of himself he could be?

A tiny insight into how his mind worked, maybe, but it would be gold for these hungry journalists.

It was gold for Ellie, too. A small nugget that she had every intention of keeping entirely to herself, although she wasn't sure why it seemed so important. She'd probably never see him again so why should it matter what he thought of her?

Ellie had always been too trusting, and she had always

been utterly trustworthy herself. Deception was anathema to her. Okay, she'd been burnt too badly to ever be as trusting again, but she'd never sink to that level.

*She* was trustworthy.

If Jake had inadvertently trusted her with even the tiniest piece of something personal and she kept that information safe, at least he would know that her integrity was intact. That she could be trusted.

And that gave her the moral high ground, didn't it? Jake might wrap it up in words that made it sound almost acceptable, but acting was a form of deception. Fine for movies when people knew that the people on screen were only characters, but he'd proved he could do it in real life, too, with that polished performance for the media.

You'd never know whether he was being honest or acting.

Did he even know himself?

In the absence of any new material, magazines were using what they could find, and to her horror the picture that appeared all over the internet, newspapers and magazines was one that had been taken just after they'd landed. When she'd seen the media falling all over Jake and Mike had been telling her who he actually was. There was no mistaking the confusion and sense of betrayal on her face. Others were passing it off as no more than a bad photo and her expression was probably due to the pain of her injured ankle, but Ellie knew the truth. She now had a permanent reminder of exactly how she'd felt in learning Jake's real identity.

She had been deceived.

*Again.*

It shouldn't have come as such a surprise. Given her experience, it should be a lot easier to deal with than last time but, somehow, this was harder. Because she'd got to a point where she'd *wanted* to trust Jake?

For the first time since the devastating betrayal of a man she'd been about to marry, Ellie had been able to see that it might be possible to fall in love again.

To trust.

Such a hard-won step forward and she'd been shoved backwards again with what felt like a cruel blow.

Whatever. She had no choice but to deal with it and get on with her life.

The extent of the battering her body had taken and the exhaustion of both the rescue and its aftermath cushioned Ellie for several days, but then she began to feel like a prisoner in her own home.

In solitary confinement.

She was totally used to living on her own. Why did she suddenly feel so lonely?

The big windows of her living area had a stunning view of the beach and the distinctive shape of Rangitoto Island—an ancient volcano. Her father's telescope still had its position at one side of the French doors that led out to the balcony and Ellie had spent a lot of time watching the activity on the stretch of water that divided Auckland harbour from the open sea. It seemed like a good way to reconnect to her own life.

To forget about Jake Logan?

Except that the bleak landscape of Rangitoto made her think about the lush rainforest cover of Half Moon Island and long to see it again. The barrier that had been there ever since her parents had been tragically killed had been forced open. It wasn't just memories of her time with Jake that were haunting Ellie now. They were competing with memories of her parents and her beloved grandfather. Happy times in a place that was a part of her soul. People that were missing from her life and had taken such big pieces of her along with them.

Everyone knew that nothing was for ever but why had she had to lose every person she had ever truly loved?

No wonder she was feeling lonely.

The usual traffic of container ships, naval vessels and ferries had been noticeably interrupted by the fleet of racing yachts when the Ultraswift-Round-the-World race was started again a few days after the cyclone and by then Ellie had to accept that it was not going to be so easy to get Jake out of her head.

It was bad enough getting reports of the way he was still touching her real life.

The helicopter rescue trust had received an impressive donation that was labelled as anonymous but it was obvious it had come from one—or both—of the Logan brothers.

Jillian, at the bird-rearing centre, was almost speechless at the size of the donation the kiwi trust had received within days of Pēpe's arrival.

'I know it's anonymous,' she told Ellie, 'but it's a bit of coincidence, wouldn't you say?'

'Lots of people care about saving kiwis. Pēpe's famous now. He was on the news.'

'Not many people can afford to care to the tune of hundreds of thousands of dollars.'

'*That* much? Phew…' Ellie closed her eyes but it didn't shut out the pictures appearing in her head. If anything, it made them clearer. The way Jake had looked as they'd watched the baby bird hatching. The way he'd looked at *her* as they'd shared that unforgettable experience.

'I did an internet search on him,' Jillian confessed. 'He's seriously hot, isn't he?'

'Bit hairy for me.'

'Have a look at some of the older photos, then, where he's clean shaven. Like back in the day when he was on *ER*. Oh, *my...*'

Ellie had to laugh. It sounded like Jillian, who was in her early sixties and had several grandchildren, was busy fanning herself.

'Amazing he's still single,' Jillian continued. 'Or maybe not. That wife of his really did a number on him, didn't she?'

'I wouldn't know. I don't read that stuff and we didn't talk about anything personal.'

They'd come close, though, hadn't they? She could still hear the bitterness in Jake's voice when he'd answered her query about him being married.

*Not anymore.*

And she'd wanted to find out. It had been a personal challenge not to search the internet and devour every piece of information she could find. The curiosity was over-powering now.

'What did she do?'

'Only went and got herself up the duff by the leading man on her first movie. A part she only got because of her connection to Jake.'

'Oh...' Ellie was stunned.

How could any woman be that *stupid?* If she'd wanted a baby she couldn't have picked a better father than Jake. Impossible not to remember how protective he'd been in trying to stop her going out into that storm. The strength he'd shown in rescuing her. How gentle he'd been in that impressive examination of her injured ankle.

'And then she dropped the bombshell online so that the whole world knew before he did.'

'That's horrible,' Ellie said, but she was backing away fast from the onslaught of emotions she didn't want to try and handle. 'Jill—I've got to go, but it's great to know how well Pēpe's doing. I'll call you again soon.'

'Okay. Speaking of calling, has *he* called you?'

'No. Why would he?' To thank her again, perhaps? With the kind of polished speech he'd given the media? What if he offered *her* money as a gesture of gratitude—or apology?

'Someone from the film company rang to ask after Pēpe the other day. A woman called Kristy or something.'

'Kirsty?'

'That's it. She asked for your phone number. Said they'd tried to get it from your work, but they wouldn't hand out personal information. Anyway, I gave her your mobile number. Hope you don't mind.'

'My phone got wrecked. I haven't got around to replacing it yet.'

'Maybe you should get a new one. And talk to him if he rings. You've got a lot in common when you come to think about it.'

'Oh…right. Like he's a famous movie star and I'm a very ordinary mortal?'

'You're on the same page as far as your love lives go.'

Ellie's snort of laughter was not amused. 'Hardly. Guess I can be grateful that it was only my friends who found out how narrowly I escaped a bigamous marriage. Far more humiliating to have the whole world devouring every detail of your betrayal.'

She didn't want to talk about Michael and, this time, she was more successful in pleading a need to end the call. Having made a note to remind herself to sort out a new phone the next day, Ellie stared at the piece of paper and then screwed it up.

What would happen if her number worked again? Would she be waiting for it to ring? Be picking it up every five minutes to see if she'd received a message? Be disappointed if it rang and it wasn't Jake on the other end?

It would be better not to risk it. In fact, when she got a new phone she'd ask for a new number as well. It would be best to forget about Jacob Logan and the way he'd managed to stir up feelings that she'd thought she was immune to. Jake needed to be tucked into the past and largely forgotten. As Michael had been.

But everything conspired to remind her, even in the seclusion of her own home. Trying to put any weight on her foot would create a throb of pain that took her back to that awful moment of finding she had been unable to walk on the beach when they'd desperately needed to find the beach house. When Jake had scooped her up into his arms and carried her to safety.

Opening her pantry to look for something to eat, the sight of canned food would take her back to that extraordinary meal by the fire.

Just needing to go to the bathroom would remind her of that terrifying moment of the tree coming down. Of Jake screaming her name as if it would be the worst thing in the world if something bad had happened to her.

The nights were even worse. There was no protection to be found from the moments that she was forced to relive in her dreams. Helping Jake take his clothes off or that almost-kiss just before that radio message had come in was always the catalyst but her unconscious mind wouldn't leave it alone. The fantasy of what could have happened if they hadn't been so uncomfortable with the situation or interrupted was played out in glorious Technicolor with the added dimension of sensations Ellie had never realised could be so powerful. More than once, she woke to find her body still pulsing with a release that left...a kind of shame in its wake.

Here she was, a thirty-two-year-old woman, mooning after a celebrity like some starstruck teenager.

It had to end.

Ellie rang her boss. 'Smithie? I'm going nuts here. I might be stuck on the ground but I really need some work to do. Can we talk?'

Jake thought he looked more like a pirate than a nine-teenth-century deckhand but that was okay. Fun, even. The baggy trousers weren't as bad as those old trackpants Ellie had given him to wear and they were tucked neatly into black leather boots that folded down at the top. The white shirt with its wide collar, laced opening and gener-ous sleeves was a bit girlie but the waistcoat hid part of it and with some artfully applied smudges of grime and a rip or two it was quite acceptable.

He eyed himself in the mirror as the makeup techni-cian started on his hair. Ellie certainly wouldn't think he was wearing his hair like this for a photo shoot as a male model, would she?

'What is that stuff?'

'Basically grease. We need that nice, dirty, dreadlocked vibe.'

'At least the bandanna hides most of it. Have to say I can't wait to get a proper haircut again.'

The makeup girl smiled at his reflection. 'I dunno… it kinda suits you. And I'm getting so used to it I almost didn't recognise you in that new article that's out.'

'Another article?' There'd been so many of them in the last few weeks that Jake didn't bother to look unless Kirsty insisted. He should be delighted that Ellie wasn't prepared to reveal anything about herself or her time with him, but perversely it was like a hurt silence that told him he'd done something wrong.

Because he hadn't trusted her?

'One of the local women's magazines. It's over there, by the wigs.'

He shouldn't have opened it. Why did they keep using that dreadful photograph of Ellie? The one where she'd clearly been told who it was that she'd rescued. When she'd realised that he had been less than honest with her. Where she looked not only as if she was in pain and exhausted but that she'd been betrayed somehow.

He'd wanted to try and explain. Of course he had. But she'd publicly turned her back on his invitation to share that press conference and she'd been unreachable ever since. Not that he'd been able to visit the rescue base where she worked in person. Or the bird sanctuary place that the baby kiwi had been taken to, but Kirsty had managed to find a phone number and he'd tried that repeatedly, only to get the message that the phone was either out of range or turned off.

How much clearer did Ellie have to make it that she didn't want anything more to do with him?

He should be over it by now. Well into the full-on work that was his career on set. They were on deadline here, with a release timed for the summer holiday season in the United States and a lot of editing, as well as special effects, that would have to be done before then. With practised focus, Jake dropped the magazine and stepped into the dark of predawn outside the caravan to begin his new day.

A good percentage of the movie was already in the can. The opening scenes with him being a surgeon with a tension-racked relationship in a high-paced American hospital before he stepped into the portal, and the ending when he was back there and trying to get to grips with normal life and able to repair the relationship thanks to what he'd faced centuries ago. There'd been scenes shot

in London, too, where he'd started to grow his hair and
beard to look the part as he got swept into employment
on an immigrant ship.

They'd had to come to New Zealand to film the guts of
the story, though, with the premise being that his medical
knowledge would save the life of a woman who would go
on to raise a child who would change history. A square-
rigged sailing ship that was going to be wrecked just off
the coast of the north island. A life-and-death struggle for
survival in the wild land of a new colony. A love story that
could never be consummated because that would have al-
tered history, but the lessons learned meant that the real-
time love story would come right.

Too ironic, really, given the experience Jake had been
through before arriving on set. The media had jumped
on that.

'How does it feel, having to be on a ship, given your
recent brush with death?'

'Safe,' Jake had told them smoothly. 'Everything that
happens here is carefully controlled. I doubt that we'll be
doing any scenes at sea if there's another cyclone forecast.'

There was medical cover, too, in case anything un-
toward happened. An ambulance was always parked
nearby, manned by volunteer officers from the nearest
local town of Whitianga on the Coromandel Peninsula.
One of them was a young woman, but thankfully she
looked nothing like Ellie. It was bad enough having the
emergency vehicle on site, reminding him every time of
the unfortunate way they'd parted.

It was just as well the female lead didn't look anything
like Ellie either. Amber was petite and redheaded, with
skin so pale it was almost transparent. And her eyes were
green, not that dark, chocolaty brown.

One of today's scenes was the first meeting of the deckhand and the immigrant girl during the arduous voyage in an overcrowded ship infested with lice, cockroaches and rats. He would be coming from a confrontation with a drunk and incompetent ship's-surgeon. She was out of the cramped, working-class cabins below deck to attend the funeral of a friend's baby who'd succumbed to typhoid fever.

That was an emotionally wrenching scene he was witness to, but being out on the water in the beautiful replica ship being used for filming was a pleasure. The sea was calm, the sunrise spectacular and the first scene of the day only needed one take.

The scene with the ship's surgeon didn't go so well. It was supposed to be a busy time for the crew, with sails being shifted to catch the wind while the argument was happening. Getting enough activity to ramp up the tension was difficult and by the third take people were tiring. During the filming, one of the extras managed to get tangled up in a rope as one of the huge sails was being lowered and he dislocated his shoulder.

It was Jake who helped carry the man to shore once the ship got back to the jetty, but the paramedic on duty wasn't qualified to administer IV pain relief. When she rang for backup, the only other ambulance in the area was out on a job.

'He'll have to be transported,' she informed the director.

He was already stressed about the hold-up in the day's filming. 'Call for a helicopter, then.'

But the closest rescue helicopter was attending a serious accident well north of Auckland and it would be over an hour before it would be available.

'I'll have to transport him myself,' the paramedic decided. 'At least I've got Entonox available.'

'How long will that take?'

'The closest hospital is in Thames. The round trip will

be at least two hours. Probably more like three, what with handing him over and roadworks and things.'

'Who's going to cover the set, then?' The director shook his head at the paramedic's expression. 'Nobody, obviously. That means we can't film.'

'Maybe one of the local doctors could come out for a bit.'

'We've got weeks of filming ahead of us. We can't afford this kind of hassle.' He looked over his shoulder towards the unfortunate extra, who was sitting on a stretcher in the back of the ambulance, Kirsty beside him, offering comfort. 'Go,' he ordered wearily. 'Get that poor guy sorted. I'm not going to make him wait.' He raised his voice. 'Kirsty? Can you come over here, please?'

'We'll have to hire independent medical cover,' was Kirsty's suggestion when she heard the tale of woe. 'Someone who's qualified to deal with any situation and give whatever treatment is needed until ground or air transport can get here. Someone who could live on site in the camping grounds with us and be available twenty-four seven.'

'How on earth are we going to find someone like that?'

'I don't know,' Kirsty admitted. 'But we do, at least, have a personal contact with the ambulance service, thanks to Jake.'

'I don't have contact, exactly,' Jake said. 'I haven't even spoken to Ellie since the rescue. The only contact was when I rang the base to see how she was a couple of weeks ago.'

It had been a last attempt to make some personal contact given that the mobile number had been such a failure. Had she really been unavailable or were her colleagues protecting her from a call from someone she didn't want to speak to?

'And how was she?'

'Getting over the ankle injury, apparently, but only on light duties. Her boss said something about her preparing teaching material. She wasn't on the base and she wouldn't be back on active duty for some time but she was fine.'

It had been a relief to know she hadn't been left with any lasting disability caused by the rescue of himself. Oddly disappointing to know that he'd have no more excuses to ask after her, though.

'Sounds perfect,' the director said. 'She's certainly qualified and not afraid of doing something different or challenging. Still got the number of her boss?'

'I have,' Kirsty said helpfully. 'His name's Smith.'

'Get him on the blower. We need to talk.'

Jake watched them walk away. It was highly unlikely that Ellie would want to take such an unusual job, even if it could be arranged, but the flare of something curiously like excitement told him that he hoped she would.

That he would get the chance to see her again.

To talk to her.

The feeling intensified as the day ticked on. Because they couldn't film without medical cover, there was too much time to think.

To feel bad that he had been less than honest with her about who he was. Had he really been worried that she might sell her story to the media? She hadn't breathed a word. She hadn't even taken the opportunity to bask in any glory associated with the dramatic rescue.

To feel frustrated, too, that he had never had the chance to try and explain anything. To apologise?

She hadn't believed him when he'd told her how acting could help you deal with real life. Maybe if she saw what really went on, she would see that it wasn't fake—not on an emotional level, anyway.

She might understand what he'd been trying to say when he'd told her something that he'd never told anybody else.

He had to admit that there was a longing there to have somebody who really understood. Ben understood his need for his career, but he still saw it all as play-acting. An escape from reality. He wasn't ever going to get close enough to the action to really get it because he hated the whole industry with such a passion.

And yet Ben had reaped the benefits of his twin's ability to act and make others believe in their early years. How often had he instigated a game that would take them away from what was happening around them?

Their lifestyle had had a veneer that was a dream to most people, but they didn't know what it was really like. A father rich enough to seemingly own half of Manhattan. A heartbreakingly beautiful mother who was loved by millions but desperately unhappy in her marriage to a bully who resented her fame.

Play-acting had been a way to escape the fights and misery and lingering bitterness. If he and Ben were pirates and they were being forced to walk the plank, the screaming row their parents were having could seem like nothing more than seagulls overhead and circling sharks below and the two small boys could poke them in the eyes and swim to safety.

All Ben could see in the industry of play-acting was the damage it had done to their mother. Their family. No wonder he hated it. And no wonder he was sticking to his unspoken vow of never repeating history. Had he ever got even as close to a woman as *he* was currently feeling about Ellie?

Ellie would probably agree wholeheartedly with Ben about the negative side of the movie industry, but…what if he could change her mind?

If someone like her could understand and maybe even approve of what he did, it could validate what he did for a living. Make him feel like he was contributing to making the world a better place.

Like Ellie did?

'That's a crazy idea.'

'A few weeks on the Coromandel Peninsula? In a nice little cabin in the camping grounds? Gorgeous weather. Probably still warm enough to swim and that would be as good for your ankle as the physiotherapy.'

'There's lots of people who'd jump at the opportunity. Why me?'

Gavin Smith grinned. 'I guess you proved yourself by saving the star of the movie once already. Maybe he asked for *you* personally.'

Why did her heart skip a beat like that? Her mouth suddenly feel unaccountably dry? Could that be true? More importantly, did she want it to be true?

Had she proved her trustworthiness by not saying anything to reporters? Did Jake realise, without knowing why, how hurt she was at having been deceived?

'I can't believe they can just click their fingers and get someone from the service who's that qualified just to sit around in case something happens.'

'New Zealand's getting a reputation as a great place to make movies. The government's keen to support the industry. The word's come from on high to provide the best we can.' Gavin raised his eyebrows encouragingly. 'That's you, Ellie.'

It was impossible not to imagine what it would be like to see Jake again. Their time together was too tangled in emotions that were partly due to the traumatic situation they'd been in. Maybe she'd get there and find that it had been nothing more than a reaction to the circumstances and that there wasn't any real attraction on either side.

And, if that was the case, maybe she could finally put the whole, disturbing episode behind her and get on with the rest of her life. It wouldn't be nibbling away at her peace of mind as it had done ever since she'd had that time with Jake.

Gavin was saying something about her being able to carry on with her current project of writing lectures about aeromedical transportation. About providing her with an extensive enough kit that she would be able to cope with any emergency with ease. That by the time she got back she'd be fully recovered and they could decide about what she wanted to do next in her career.

But all Ellie could think about was being close to Jake again. Would he look at her again the way he had in that moment before they'd almost kissed?

'Okay…' Her voice came out in a whisper. 'I'll do it.'

# CHAPTER EIGHT

THE DRIVE FROM Auckland to the Coromandel township of Whitianga only took two and half hours, but it was enough time for Ellie to have a good think about how she was going to handle the moment when she and Jake met again.

It was ironic that she was joining a film crew and would be on set while a movie was being filmed because the only way she was going to be able to cope with this was to become something of an actress herself.

Well...she could hardly reveal to the world that she—an ordinary Kiwi girl—had some kind of mixed-up crush on a famous movie star, could she? How humiliating would that be?

And she had been humiliated before. She wasn't going there again.

Funny how Jake's words kept echoing in her head during that drive. And it was definitely motivating to imagine watching herself on the big screen here. Cheering herself on. Facing obstacles and overcoming them.

*Practising being the best person she could be, even if it felt like the skin didn't fit yet.*

She would be pleased to see him—as she would be to catch up on any of the patients she'd rescued during her career. Keen to do something so different. Excited, even, to be part of a totally new world.

She would realise that the crush was no more than the aftermath of an overly emotional situation and that there was nothing real to hang any fantasies on. She would re-affirm her faith that dealing with reality was preferable to trying to escape and then she would go back to her own life, with her head held high, to do exactly that.

The autumn weather was stunning as she wound her way through over the mountain range and through the small township of Tairua. Beneath a cloudless blue sky, the lush native forest looked cool and green and the glimpses of ocean a bottomless blue. The main holiday season was well over so Whitianga was quiet, but there was a buzz of excitement in the air that Ellie noticed when she stopped for a few supplies and directions to the camping grounds. That, and her uniform, earned her a curious glance from the shopkeeper.

'Someone been hurt again?'

'Again?' The pang of concern that it could be Jake came from nowhere and the way Ellie could feel her eyes widening was disturbing. She'd never make an actress if she couldn't keep her reactions under better control.

'Someone broke their arm a couple of days ago. Or was it their shoulder? Anyway…they had to stop filming for a day. Did you know they're doing a movie here? Have you seen the boat at the marina?'

'I did. It's beautiful.'

'They're going to do a shipwreck scene round at Cathedral Cove in the next week or two. There's places that people are allowed to go and watch.'

'Sounds fun.'

Her items were being slotted into a carrier bag. 'So no one else has been hurt, then?'

'Not that I know of.'

'But that's why you're here?'

'I'm here to give some first-aid cover.' Ellie practised the kind of smile she would use for a reporter, perhaps, who wanted information. 'Hopefully just as an insurance policy. Can you tell me where the local ambulance station is, too? I'll drop in and say hi on my way.'

She was here.

The SUV painted in ambulance insignia, with the beacon strip on its roof, stood out as clearly as if the lights had been flashing, when Jake emerged from the makeup caravan. The director, Steve, was obviously showing her around the camping ground, along with Kirsty and the camp manager.

Jake could feel his heart rate pick up. The kind of warmth in his chest that he'd only ever noticed when he saw his brother after a longer than usual period apart.

Relief, that's what it was. Mixed with joy. And…hope?

She looked very professional in a crisp, white shirt that had epaulettes and patches on the sleeves. Dark trousers and a belt that had things clipped to it, like a pair of shears and some sort of radio or phone. Her black boots were shining. So was the rope of neatly plaited hair that hung down her back.

Another image flashed into his head. Ellie, sitting in front of the fire, in shapeless trackpants and a checkered woollen shirt, her hair loose and tumbling as she raked her fingers through it.

He preferred that image…

He wished he wasn't in full costume and makeup himself because he was going to look as different to Ellie as she did to him and it felt…wrong.

She didn't even seem to recognise him as her gaze swept around and past where he was standing motionless. But then Steve spotted him.

'Here's someone you'll remember,' he heard the director say. 'Not that there's much time for a catch-up. I'm sorry. We're due to head down to the ship in a couple of minutes.'

'Jake…' Ellie's smile was wide and friendly. She was holding out her hand and when he caught it, the handshake was firm and brief. 'It's so good to see you again.' The smile was directed at the others in the group now. 'It's a bonus you don't often get in my job—catching up with the patients that get rescued.'

Jake blinked. He was a *patient?* Just one of the dozens—or possibly hundreds—that Ellie had rescued in her career?

'Great that you could come,' he heard himself saying. 'I didn't think we'd be lucky enough to get our first choice.' He was smiling, too. He wanted Ellie to know that he'd wanted it to be her. Had wanted to see her again.

'How could I say no?' The smile hadn't dimmed. In fact, it got wider. 'This is a once-in-a-lifetime opportunity for me. How many people get the chance to be part of what's no doubt going to be a blockbuster movie? I'm hoping you're all going to stay nice and safe and it'll work out as a holiday treat for me.'

'Hear! Hear!' Steve muttered.

'Not that I'm not fully equipped to deal with any emergency,' Ellie added hastily. 'My car is full to the brim with everything from sticky plasters to a portable ventilator.'

'And with your connection to the helicopter service, I'm sure we'd get priority treatment.' Kirsty nodded.

Ellie's smile faded only a notch. 'Doesn't work like that, I'm afraid. No preferential treatment because of who you are.'

Jake couldn't read the glance flicked in his direction, but it had been impersonal and there was something about the inflection in her words that struck a cool enough note to send a tiny shiver down his spine.

And then it hit him.

This wasn't Ellie talking. Not the *real* Ellie.

She was…*acting,* dammit. Saying the things that were presenting the image she'd chosen to present.

The way *he* had the last time they'd been breathing the same air, at that media conference in The Cloud? When he'd been putting all that warmth and gratitude into his pretty little speech about how good the New Zealand rescue services were and about one paramedic in particular? Had he really gushed on about his 'real-life heroine'?

This felt like a slap in the face. Payback.

But that wasn't Ellie either. Not the Ellie he remembered, anyway.

'Come on, Jake. Time to get to work.' Steve thumped him on the shoulder as he headed off. 'Kirsty will bring Ellie down to the set once she's had a look at her cabin and got herself sorted.'

With a nod at the women, Jake was happy to comply. Maybe it had been a mistake, getting Ellie here.

He certainly wasn't feeling any of that warmth or joy or hope of special moments to come anymore. The emotion he was left with after that little reunion was more like wariness. Dread, even, that Ellie might have more planned as some kind of revenge.

No. Someone as open and honest and caring as Ellie wouldn't even think like that. He knew her better than that.

Didn't he?


He'd seen straight through her.

And Ellie felt ashamed of herself.

The warmth in Jake's eyes when he'd seen her had been genuine, but Ellie had already been locked into her role

as the caring and professional medic who just happened
to have rescued one of the stars of this movie and she had
been unable to find any middle ground between that image
and the stupid, starstruck teenager with a crush she'd been
scared of revealing.

She'd seen the moment he'd twigged that she was acting. Had seen his surprise and then the flash of something
that had looked remarkably like hurt.

So now she felt bad.

It didn't take long for the camp manager to show her the
tiny cabin that would be hers for the duration of her stay.
Or to give her a bag of coins and explain about the showers.

'You get five minutes of hot water for one dollar. Just
put another coin in if you need longer. The company's
paying all those costs so I've got lots of coins available.'

Ellie nodded.

'The caterers have taken over the main kitchen areas
and they've been putting on some amazing barbecues.
You'll get well fed.'

'Excellent.' Ellie managed another smile but the churn-
ing sensation in her gut made her think she might never
feel hungry again.

'Well, I won't hold you up. You probably can't wait to
get down to the set and see what's going on. I'd kill for a
chance to spend my day watching Jake Logan.' The mid-
dle-aged woman grinned at Ellie. 'If I was twenty years
younger, he wouldn't stand a chance. Okay…make that
thirty years. But you know what I'm saying?'

Ellie nodded politely.

'I'd be in a long queue, mind you. And it's not as if
anything lasts in Tinseltown, but it would sure be fun for
a while, wouldn't it?'

'Mmm.' Ellie couldn't manage to sound remotely en-
thusiastic. Of course Jake would have a queue of women

happy to take their turn, even knowing how temporary that would be.

She wouldn't be joining any queue.

The camp manager gave up on having a girlie chat. 'Just knock on the office door, love, if you need anything.'

'Okay. Thank you.'

She wasn't in as much of a hurry to get to the set as the camp manager had assumed, however. She wasn't even sure if she wanted to be near Jake again so soon. She'd snuffed out the warmth she'd seen in his face in that re-union.

There was no use dressing it up as self-protection. The truth was she'd snubbed him and he'd known. Someone like Jake Logan didn't have to bother with people who snubbed him. He could just pick one of those willing women in the queue. If she never saw even a hint of that warmth again, she only had herself to blame.

That she'd made a bad mistake and that things could have gone very differently haunted Ellie for the rest of that first day.

Her nose was rubbed in it, in fact, by being allowed on the ship during the early evening to watch a sunset scene being filmed on the gentle roll of the open sea just outside the harbour.

A kiss scene between Jake and his stunningly beautiful leading lady, Amber.

Bad enough to have to watch it once but, for some reason, the director made them do it over and over again. And Ellie was forced to watch. Not only was she trapped on a ship but she couldn't even slip out of sight because the area of the deck not being used for the scene was so small that she and the other people watching were hemmed into a corner.

The clapboards came down again and again as another take began.

Ellie had to grit her teeth. She had no hope of controlling the stirring of feelings like longing. Envy, possibly. Just as well nothing had really happened between her and Jake. Imagine having to watch this if you were in a real relationship with one of them?

'Couldn't see what was wrong with the last one,' someone close to Ellie muttered.

A snort of mirth came from someone else. 'Maybe they're enjoying it too much.'

Jealousy was such a destructive emotion. She had no right to be edging dangerously close to feeling that herself. No right at all and she would be wise to remember that.

The director went in to talk to them at this point. He waved his arm, indicating the last of the glorious sunset gilding the water behind them and throwing the slopes of tree-covered land in the distance into soft silhouette. Maybe he said something about time being money and it was running out because Jake turned and took a couple of paces as if suppressing frustration.

'Places, please,' came the call for a new take. 'Picture is up.'

Jake turned back and it felt as if he'd known all along exactly where Ellie was standing.

For a long, long, moment he simply stared at her, his face completely expressionless.

And then the assistant director called for quiet, the sound crew confirmed they were ready and a now-familiar bark of 'Action!' was heard. The new take started and it felt to Ellie like she, along with the rest of the world, had been completely shut out.

Amber was his sole focus. Kissing her was something Jake couldn't avoid any more than taking his next breath. It was inevitable. As necessary to life as the oxygen around him.

The cameras were gliding in for a close-up, but Ellie felt like she was too close already. She could feel the intensity of every moment of that long, long kiss. Could feel Jake looking at Amber in exactly the way he'd looked at her in the moments before that radio message had interrupted them. She could actually *feel* his lips getting closer. Touching...

Dear Lord... How far did they go in a movie kiss? Were their tongues touching?

Desire was still there. She could feel it curling—almost exploding—deep in her own belly. Ellie didn't dare look at anyone near her in case they could see what she was feeling in her face. Not that she could look away from the kissing couple, anyway.

Until, finally, it was over.

'That's the one,' the director shouted. 'Thanks, guys. It was *perfect*.'

The caterers, once again, had done an impressive job with the barbecue dinner laid on for cast and crew when the day's filming was over. The array of meat and fish was complemented by numerous salads and fresh, crusty bread. Wine and beer were freely available at the table set up as a bar and clusters of people were enjoying the alfresco meal as stars glittered in an inky sky above.

Jake had used a handful of coins with the time it took to get rid of his makeup and hair product. Dressed in black jeans and a matching sweater, he set out to look for food.

And Ellie.

Time was a luxury because the meeting to watch the dailies of today's footage would be on before long and he needed to collect the next day's shooting schedule, but if he didn't do something about this, it was going to do his head in. For the first time in his life he'd felt self-conscious on set this evening. It was no wonder they'd had to do that kiss scene so many times. It had been impossible to get in the zone with Ellie standing there, *watching* him.

Either they needed to clear the air between them or he'd have to ask for her to be kept off set and he could imagine the awkward questions that might result from that request. It would, no doubt, get back to Ellie too, and that would only exacerbate any ill feeling that was there.

He spotted her, standing to one side of the large group of people, looking a little uncertain. She had changed out of her uniform and, like him, was wearing jeans. She might find that camisole top wasn't enough for the chill the evenings could offer later, but even as Jake had the thought he saw Ellie push her arms into the sleeves of an oversized cardigan that draped gracefully, like a kind of shawl. She might be feeling out of place here, but she still held herself tall, confident in her independence.

The cast and crew were predominantly male. Actors, stuntpeople, camera crews, sound technicians, the grip crew, the continuity guys and others. Yeah... There were a lot of men here and Ellie was a very beautiful young woman. She wouldn't be standing alone for long, that was for sure.

Snagging a bottle of lager and a glass of wine, Jake headed in her direction. He held the glass up as he got closer as if it could pass as a peace offering.

But Ellie shook her head. 'I might be out of uniform for the night but I'm on duty twenty-four seven,' she told him.

No chance that a drink might ease the atmosphere, then.

'Doesn't sound like much fun.'

Ellie's smile was bright. Too bright. 'I'm loving it so far,' she said. 'I've never been on a movie set before. Can't believe how lucky I am to score this gig. Guess I have you to thank for that?'

Jake said nothing. He was staring at her, but Ellie was looking around. At everyone except him.

'I didn't think you'd want to come,' he said quietly.

'Hey…' Her gaze brushed past his fleetingly. 'This is my chance. Who knows—the fame might rub off on me. Someone will spot me doing my job and Hollywood might be calling with a role for a paramedic in some upcoming movie.'

That did it. Jake's voice was quiet but cool. 'If you'd wanted fame, you could have had it in spades by now. You must have had any number of chances to get your picture in magazines and all over the internet by now. Why didn't you take them?'

That threw her. He managed to catch her gaze this time. And hold it. He could actually see the way she was searching for a new line. A plausible way of covering the real reason.

He almost smiled. She'd never make an actress, the way her feelings played out over her face like that. Unless she could tap into them, of course, and use them when she needed to. Like he did.

When he saw the softening in her eyes he knew that the real reason she hadn't acceded to the media's demands was because of…what was it…loyalty? To *him*?

What had he done to deserve that? Now was the time to thank her for respecting his privacy. To apologise. Explain and put things right. But even as he took a breath he could see Ellie's expression changing again. Getting distant. She had found something to hide behind.

'That would have been more like *shame* than fame,' she said. 'D'you think I wanted the whole world knowing what an idiot I was for not recognising you?'

Jake raised an eyebrow. 'I was in disguise.'

'You told me your *name*.'

'So? It's just a name. Have you ever done an internet search on yourself and found how many people in the world have the same name as you?'

'Fine.' But Ellie wasn't going to accept an excuse. 'Maybe I didn't want to come across as some uncultured slob who never watches movies.'

It was nowhere near the truth and Jake wasn't getting anywhere. Moving so fast Ellie had no time to prepare a defence, he discarded the drinks he was holding and grabbed her hand. Never mind if he missed seeing the dailies. He could catch up later. This was more important.

'Come with me,' he ordered.

She had no choice. It was lucky she'd been standing where she was, not only on the outskirts of the group but almost beside a track that Jake knew led to the beach. Intent on their meals and downtime, no one saw them slip away.

'What the—?' Ellie was resisting the firm grip on her hand and the way Jake was pulling her forward. 'Where are you taking me?'

'The beach.'

'Why?'

'We need to talk.' The words were clipped. 'Somewhere private.'

He felt her resistance ebb. By the time they reached the beach it almost felt like Ellie was happy to hold his hand, but it was harder going in the soft sand. When they got to the firmer sand close to where the gentle waves were slowly curling onto land, she gave a tug that made Jake let go.

'My shoes are full of sand.' She pulled off the canvas sneakers and emptied them but didn't put them back on. Instead, she rolled up her jeans as far as her knees and walked out far enough to let the foamy water cover her feet and ankles.

'Bit of sea water's just as good as a session of physio,' she said.

Jake closed his eyes and groaned. 'I didn't think. I'm sorry. There I was pulling you along that rough track and I didn't even ask how your ankle was.'

'It's fine. And this is nice. The water's delicious. You should try it.'

There was something different about Ellie's voice. She sounded more like the Ellie who Jake remembered.

And the suggestion sounded more like a peace offering than he'd managed with that unwanted glass of wine. Jake toed off his shoes, but he couldn't get his jeans any further than the swell of his calves. He walked into the water, anyway, uncaring when the first tiny wave soaked the denim.

For a while they simply walked together, listening to the wash of the sea. Smelling the fresh air and looking up at the deepening blanket of stars. The moon was rising now, but the pale light didn't dim the night sky.

And it was perfect. Even alone with his brother, Jake had never felt this…peaceful…in the company of another person. Able to be exactly who he was and know he would be accepted for that.

Liked, even?

Maybe. He had a bit of work to do first.

It was Jake who finally broke the silence. 'The sky never looked like this in New York. I grew up not even realising how many stars there are out there. I grew up without the chance to realise a lot of other important things, too.'

He waited out the hesitation in Ellie's response. 'Such as?'

'That who you are doesn't mean as much as *what* you are.'

Ellie stopped walking. Jake could feel her puzzled look behind him. He stopped too, and turned back.

'I grew up as Rita Marlene's kid,' he told her. 'That won't mean much to you but—'

'I know who she is,' Ellie interrupted him. 'Everybody knows who she is...*was*. She's up there with Brigitte Bardot and Marilyn Monroe. One of the world's most beautiful women.'

'And she was married to my father. Charles Logan. One of New York's most powerful men. There wasn't anybody who didn't want to get close to one or both of my parents. Getting their kids to get friendly with the Logan kids was a goldmine.'

Ellie said nothing but he could tell she was listening.

'I didn't mean to get into acting as a career,' he continued. 'I just sort of fell into it when Ben and I got back from Afghanistan. Well...after I got rehabilitated, that is. The opening was always there, thanks to who my mother was, and it seemed like a fun thing to try for a while. More fun than Ben was having, being responsible and getting into the family business anyway. So I took that part in *ER* and then it just snowballed.'

'Mmm...' Ellie was still standing there, letting the waves soak her ankles.

'What I'm trying to say, in a roundabout way, is that I didn't tell you who I was because I had the chance to be someone nobody else ever sees. *Myself.*'

The moon was bright enough for Jake to see Ellie's face so clearly he could swear her eyes were shining with unshed tears. He allowed his gaze to travel over her features. That glorious hair. The proud way she held her head. She was *such* a beautiful woman.

'I thought...I thought it was because you didn't trust me.'

'We were complete strangers,' he pointed out. 'Thrown together by extraordinary circumstances. We were trying to survive in what felt like the middle of nowhere and I was worried sick about Ben. Did *you* trust me?'

The hesitation was there again. 'Y-yes,' Ellie finally said. 'After you carried me along the beach like that? And after you rescued me from under that tree?' Her lips wobbled slightly. 'I…trusted you.'

'Past tense?' Maybe they were clearing the air here, but could they get back to what it had been like between them? It was only now that Jake realised how much he wanted that.

'I…' He could see the muscles in Ellie's throat working as she swallowed. 'I don't really let myself trust anyone these days.'

'Why not?'

The silence went on too long this time and Jake had no right to push. He could respect her need for privacy. It didn't need to stop him being honest.

'Not trusting you *was* part of it, I guess,' he admitted. 'But that was something I *did* learn as I grew up. A lesson that's only been hammered in a lot deeper in recent years. The only person I've ever been able to trust completely is my brother Ben.' Jake flinched as a higher wave splashed the back of his legs. Or was it because of the thought he couldn't repress? 'And I can't even trust Ben now.'

'Why not?'

He could have followed Ellie's lead and simply stayed silent, but he chose not to. 'Because he lied to me.'

'What about?'

Jake couldn't help looking around but they were alone on the beach. Two dark figures, late at night. They were probably virtually invisible.

'If I tell you,' he said softly, 'you'll know I'm trusting you. *Really* trusting you.'

And maybe this was the most sincere apology he could

offer. He saw Ellie nod, but he also saw her slight shiver. Anticipation? Or was she cold?

He held out his hand and this time she took it willingly. He led her up towards the softer sand that still held the warmth of the day's sun and, although he let go of her hand when they sat down, they were still sitting close enough to touch.

For a long time he couldn't find the words to start. It was too big and by telling it to someone else it was going to make it real. But Jake had forgotten how he'd met Ellie, hadn't he?

'I heard him yelling at you,' Ellie said quietly. 'When you were both arguing about who got to get rescued first. I heard him say "Why do you think she killed herself?" Is that what this is about?'

Jake's nod was jerky. 'I didn't know. I've always believed it was an accidental overdose.'

'Who was he talking about?'

'Our mother.'

'Oh….*Jake*…' This time it was Ellie who reached for *his* hand. 'That's horrible.'

'It's believable, though.' Jake's voice was raw. 'Looking back, I can see she was an alcoholic, but who wouldn't be, married to my father? He was a bully. A complete bastard, if I'm honest. And she was dependent on prescription meds. The media used to describe her as being "beautiful but fragile" and that hit the nail on the head. But…I thought she loved us. That she wouldn't choose to leave us alone with our father.'

'Of course she loved you.' Ellie's tone was fierce. 'But sometimes that's not enough. And sometimes people convince themselves that the ones they love will be better off without them, however wrong that is. How…how old were you?'

'Fourteen.'

'Young enough to still think it was somehow your fault.'

'Except I didn't. Because I didn't know it was suicide. Ben kept that to himself.'

'He loves you, too. He was protecting you.'

The words were simple.

And Jake could feel the truth of them. There was only a twenty-minute difference in age but Ben had always had the mindset of an older brother. The more responsible one. The more protective one.

Ben had been the one to spend a night in jail after one of their worst teenage pranks, hot-wiring the Lamborghini belonging to one of their father's guests and then crashing it. He himself had been safely out of the way, admitted to hospital overnight thanks to the concussion he'd suffered.

They'd never talked about that night either. Because it had been the next morning that their mother had been found dead?

And, while Jake had been the one with the more visible injury after that dreadful incident in Afghanistan, it had been Ben who'd really been traumatised. *He* had been unconscious after the bomb blast. He had no memory of it. Ben was the one who'd been in the midst of the carnage. Trying to keep his brother alive amidst the screams of dying children.

His brother had retreated into being even more responsible after that, finally—reluctantly—picking up the reins of their father's empire when the old man had been felled by a stroke, whereas *he* had just kept having fun. With easy access to the first rungs of a Hollywood career thanks to the legacy of their famous actress mother, his own talent at making others believe combined with what the glossy magazines called his raw sex appeal had ensured a meteoric rise to stardom.

The brothers had drifted apart in the intervening years and maybe he had been harbouring resentment about the way Ben viewed the movie industry. In the light of what he'd said about their mother, though, it was far more understandable.

Was there a way back?

It had taken Ellie to point out what should have been obvious all along. Maybe she was wise enough to have some other answers.

'Why can't he tell me that himself? *Talk* to me?'

'You'll have to ask him that yourself. But he's a bloke.' Ellie slanted him a look that was pure woman. 'You lot have trouble talking about feelings.'

'Yeah...'

'And speaking of feelings, I'm kind of hungry.'

'Me, too.'

'Shall we go back and see if there's any food left?'

'Sure.' Jake got to his feet and offered Ellie his hand to help her up. He held onto it for a moment longer. 'Friends again?' he asked softly. 'Am I forgiven?'

'Of course. And thank you for trusting me. I won't let you down.'

'I know that.'

He did. And the knowledge gave him the feeling of finding something very rare and precious.

Trust was a good foundation for friendship. Better than good. The fizzing sensation of unexpected happiness was magic. A bit like being drunk. Maybe that was why he opened his mouth and kept talking as they entered the darkness of the bush track that led back to the camping ground.

'I hope tomorrow's not such a long day. I couldn't believe how many times I stuffed up that last scene.'

Ellie's voice was a little tight. 'I heard the director say that it was perfect in the end, though.'

'You want to know why?'

They were almost back at the barbecue area. They could hear the sound of voices and laughter. Their private time was almost over.

And Ellie was looking up at him, her eyes wary.

'Why?'

'Because I stopped being aware that you were watching me.'

'I was putting you off?' Ellie sounded horrified. 'Maybe I shouldn't be on set, then.'

'No. It was good that you were there. That's how I got it right in the end.'

She was puzzled again now. Jake felt like he might be stepping over a precipice right now, but he'd gone this far. He couldn't stop now.

And maybe it was a cheesy thing to say and Ellie would think it was some kind of line, but Jake realised he'd been needing to do more than apologise. He needed to let Ellie know that the time they'd had together had been special. That he wished he *had* kissed her back in that beach house. Before she'd known who he was. When he'd just been being himself.

'I just had to take myself back in time a bit,' he said softly. 'I imagined that we'd never heard that radio message. And that Amber was you.'

Once again, Ellie had been stopped in her tracks by something Jake had said.

She didn't have the wash of sea water around her ankles this time and she wasn't at all puzzled by these words. There was no mistaking the meaning this time.

Jake was telling her that he'd wanted to kiss her when

he'd had the opportunity. As much as she had wanted him to?

He hadn't forgotten the moment anyway. Any more than she had.

Beyond Jake, she could see the lights and movement of the large group of people they were about to rejoin. She could smell the tantalising aroma of roasted meat, but her hunger for food had evaporated. Here, on this unlit track through the trees, she and Jake were still alone. Unseen.

On her first day on this job, Ellie had achieved what she'd hoped she might. Time with Jake Logan that had eliminated any sense of being deceived or betrayed.

Was she just being gullible, falling for that idea that she'd given him some kind of precious gift by allowing him to be simply himself and not a household name or the son of famous people?

How could she not believe it? Especially when he'd gone on to share what had gone wrong in his relationship with his brother. That was the kind of story a journalist would kill for and Jake had *trusted* her with that information.

That was enough to give her the closure she'd wanted, wasn't it? To turn that experience into something positive that she could remember with pleasure in years to come.

But...Jake was looking at her now, the way he had in all those secret fantasies she'd indulged in during some of the long nights in the last few weeks. As if every word he'd uttered this evening had come straight from the heart and she was special to him.

Special enough to want to be more than friends.

And, heaven help her, Ellie knew without a shadow of doubt in that moment that she was in love with Jake. She had been, ever since that moment he'd gone into the hole beneath the tree roots to rescue a kiwi egg for her. She might have buried the realisation because of what had come next, but she had nothing to bury it with now.

There it was. Newly hatched and exposed. Making Ellie feel vulnerable in a way she'd sworn never to let herself feel again. So vulnerable she could actually feel herself trembling. Had she really told him that she'd trusted him?

And meant it?

Yes… She'd not only reclaimed that step forward in her life, there was a part of her doing a victory dance on the new patch of ground.

Even if nothing was showing on her face, it was going to be a mission to try and disguise that trembling. Unless she said something about how cold it was getting?

She had to say something. She couldn't stand here all night staring at Jake as though the world had stopped spinning.

But it was Jake who moved. Stepping closer without breaking the eye contact that was holding Ellie prisoner.

That on-screen kiss must have been merely a practice session because this one was a thousand percent better. The way he touched her face with reverent fingers, still holding her gaze as if reading something printed on her soul. The infinite slowness with which he lowered his head. The sweet torture of his lips hovering so close to her own she could feel the warmth of them and a buzz of sensation that went through every cell of her body.

And then his fingers slid into her hair and cradled the back of her head as the whisper of touch danced and then settled. As her lips parted beneath his and she felt the first, intimate touch of his tongue, Ellie knew she was lost.

The world really had stopped spinning.

# CHAPTER NINE

BY TACIT AGREEMENT, no direct mention was made about whatever was growing between Ellie and Jake. They both knew it was there and it was getting bigger every day. Perhaps trying to confine it to words would put it at risk of being caged and stunt its growth. Or maybe, by acknowledging it, it would somehow make it visible to others. This was theirs alone and it was too fragile and precious to put at risk.

Keeping it secret became a game that only added excitement to the stakes as they went about the jobs they were paid to do. Jake had to spend hours in makeup and costume, learning his lines and filming scene after scene as the movie inched towards the major finale of the shipwreck. Ellie treated people for minor and sometimes moderate injuries and illnesses. A cameraman needed a night in hospital to check that his chest pain wasn't cardiac related. One of the catering crew got a nasty burn and someone else had an asthma attack that kept her busy for some time.

She'd never known that an ignition point of sexual tension could be stretched *so* far. One day led to another and then another where nothing happened other than an apparently innocent conversation over a meal, a lingering glance during the hours of a working day or, at best, a stolen moment of physical contact that was unlikely to arouse anyone's suspicion—like the brush of hands as Jake passed her a plate of food or a drink.

The movie's star didn't really need the skills of a highly qualified paramedic to tend to the small scratch he received after a fight scene. It wasn't very professional of Ellie either to spend quite so much time assessing and cleaning the insignificant wound but the time in the caravan set aside as an on-set clinic was as private as they'd been since that walk on the beach and that seemed so long ago it was getting shrouded in the same mists of fantasy that Ellie's dreams were.

As she used a piece of gauze to dry the skin on Jake's neck that she'd cleaned so thoroughly, the swiftness of his movement when he caught her wrist startled her.

'I'm going mad,' he said softly. 'I need some time with you. Away from this crowd. Or any of those nosy reporters.'

Oh…my… Ellie knew exactly what would happen if they were really alone again. Like they had been in the beach house.

Did she want that, too?

Oh…yeah… With every fibre of her being.

Even if a part of her knew perfectly well it couldn't last? That her world was so different from Jake's she knew she could never fit in and that, if she allowed herself to go any further down this alluring path, it had to end in tears?

*Her* tears?

But it was so easy to blot out the future and live in the moment. To view this interlude in her life as a one-off and that, if this was the only time she would ever have to be with Jake, it would be worth it. Yes. If the invitation was there, she could no more stop herself going down that path than stop breathing for a week.

The time it had taken to reach that conclusion had been

no more than the time it had taken Ellie to suck in a long breath, but it was enough for wariness to cloud Jake's eyes. He kept his voice low enough for no one to overhear, even if they were right outside the slightly open door of the caravan.

'Do you want that, too, Ellie? Is it only me that's going crazy, here? Would you rather—?'

Ellie stilled his words with her finger on his lips. She looked over her shoulder to ensure they were alone and then she used the tip of her finger to trace the outline of Jake's lips. When she felt the touch of his tongue against her fingertip she had to close her eyes. Stifle the tiny cry that escaped her own lips.

It was the only answer Jake needed.

'I'm overdue for a bit of down time. A day off. We could go somewhere. I've got a chopper available. We could go anywhere we liked.'

'Wouldn't it be rather obvious what we were doing?'

The media had been trying to link Jake romantically with Amber and it hadn't stuck. They'd have a field day if he took off to an unknown destination with the on-set paramedic, who just happened to be the mysterious woman he'd been confined in a remote cabin with for two days.

Unless…

'What if we went to visit Pēpe? That would be a legit-imate reason to go somewhere together. A photo op for you, even. I'm sure Jillian would love the publicity that it would give the bird-rearing centre.'

'And then…?' Jake was smiling. He loved the idea. Ex-citement had Ellie's blood fizzing like champagne and a million butterflies were dancing in her stomach.

'If we've got the use of a chopper we could go any-where.' She was on a roll here. 'We could buy some cans of spaghetti and restock the pantry at the beach house.'

You couldn't get more private than that. Especially if they sent the chopper away for an hour or three.

'You...' Jake was still holding the wrist he'd caught. He pulled Ellie's hand to his lips and pressed a kiss to the palm of her hand. '...are brilliant. I'll talk to Steve today. We're going to make this happen. Soon.'

'You almost done in there, Jake?' A crew member didn't bother knocking as he stuck his head in the door. 'Make-up's waiting to make you beautiful again.'

'All good.' Jake dropped Ellie's hand as if it was red hot. 'On my way.'

She hid her face by dropping to pick up the piece of gauze that had fallen, unnoticed, to the floor but looked up as Jake reached the door. The glance he sent over his shoulder said it all.

'Soon' couldn't be soon enough.

It was Kirsty who persuaded Steve that the publicity the visit would engender would make it more than worthwhile to give Jake a day off.

Unfortunately, she also insisted that she go too.

'I'm organising the coverage,' she told him. 'Setting up the interviews. I *have* to be there.'

'Look...' Jake tried to keep a note of desperation out of his voice. 'I was planning a little surprise for Ellie. The place we were when she rescued me is close to an island where her grandfather used to be the lighthouse keeper. I wanted to use the chopper to take her there to see it again. As a...a thank-you, I guess, for what she did for me. I hadn't planned on having a...a...'

'Chaperone?' Kirsty's glance was amused. And knowing.

'It's not like that.' Good grief... He was good at this acting lark. He could channel his frustration into injecting just the right note of irritation here to put Kirsty off the track. 'Would you want to swap your stilettos for trainers so you could go tramping around on an uninhabited island for a few hours, looking for native birds?'

'Heavens, no.' Kirsty was horrified. 'But I do need to do the media wrangling.' She raised an eyebrow. 'And wouldn't that make it seem more like what it is? Just a visit to somewhere that you both happen to have an interest in visiting?'

She was right. The more official it was, the less likely it would be that Ellie would start getting hounded by reporters or chased by the paparazzi. He had to protect her from that at all costs because, if anything was going to kill what was happening between them, it would be the relentless intrusion of the media and the way they could blow things up out of all proportion and offer their own twisted motivations for whatever was happening in a relationship. Ellie would hate that even more than Ben did and it would undoubtedly be a deal-breaker.

Maybe it could still work. He just had to come up with a way of making sure it did.

It was hard to tell whether Jillian was more thrilled by the attention the centre was receiving or by meeting Jake Logan. Everybody, including Kirsty, was delighted with how the morning went.

Jillian got to talk about the centre.

'Captive rearing centres like this are vital to the survival of our iconic native kiwis. Especially the endangered ones like Pēpe, who's a rare brown kiwi. Out in the wild, a chick has about a five percent chance of making it to adulthood. The ones we hatch and rear here have more like a sixty-five percent chance. We need support to do our work, though. We rely on public contributions as much as government funding.'

The small army of photographers and television crews loved the shots of Jake holding Pēpe. Having been told what a rare privilege it was, Jake was loving it too. His smile had camera shutters clicking madly and the reporter interviewing him couldn't help the occasional coo of appreciation.

'So he's due to be released soon? Will you want to be a part of that occasion, too?'

'If it's possible, I would consider it an honour.'

Ellie was more than happy to stay in the background. She was the link between the film star and the new poster bird for the centre and that was enough.

Having coached Jake on how to hold the bird by the legs with one hand so he wasn't in danger of being scratched and cradling the bird's body in the crook of his other arm, Jillian stood aside with her friend as they watched Jake being interviewed.

'You're right,' Jillian whispered. 'Too much hair.'

'He gets to cut it all off after they do the big shipwreck scene. He says he can't wait.'

'Does he, now?' Jillian's voice was a murmur. 'And what's with this threesome business on your day off? Did he have anything to say about that?'

'Apparently he has a plan.'

Something in her tone must have revealed more than Ellie had intended because Jillian's eyes widened.

'Oh…*my*…' she whispered. Then a shadow dimmed her smile. 'Be careful, won't you, hon?'

'Maybe I need to stop being so careful,' Ellie whispered back. 'This is too good to lose and…and I think I can trust him.'

'I hope so.' But there was concern in Jillian's eyes now. 'I don't want you getting hurt again.'

* * *

Ellie didn't know what Jake's plan was, any more than she knew what was in the basket that the caterers had given Jake to store in the helicopter. When they took off and headed north of Auckland after the visit to Pēpe, her heart sank. She assumed the basket was full of tinned food for the beach house and it looked as if Kirsty was coming with them. But as they got close the helicopter veered away from the shore and began to lose altitude.

'Oh, look…' Kirsty said. 'It's the lighthouse. And there's another house, too. Is that where we're going to land?'

Nobody answered her. Ellie was still too astonished to speak when the chopper touched down on the long grass of a small clearing between the lighthouse and the keeper's cottage. She didn't need the instruction to keep her head down as Jake helped her out but she did wonder why the engine wasn't being shut down. Jake followed her, carrying the basket and then he raised an arm and the helicopter took off again.

With Kirsty still inside it.

'He'll be back by four p.m.,' Jake told her. 'He's going to drop Kirsty off and refuel and have some lunch.' He raised the basket. 'This is our lunch. I hope the champagne's still cold.'

Ellie's jaw dropped. 'I thought it was full of cans of spaghetti.'

'Spaghetti's strictly for emergencies,' Jake told her. 'This was carefully planned.' His smile faded and he looked solemn. 'This is just for us, Ellie. Kirsty's job would be on the line if she said anything and the pilot's too well paid not to be trusted. We can restock the beach house another time.'

He was already planning another time? Ellie's joy—and her smile—expanded another notch. 'I can't believe I'm here. Standing on Half Moon Island. I haven't been here since…for ever. Are you sure it's okay? Did you check with the owners?'

'Owners? I thought it was government property.'

'I'm not sure now. It was put up for sale a few years ago, but I never heard whether anyone bought it.'

'It was for sale?'

Ellie smiled. 'A snip at only a few million. Pretty pricey for a holiday house with no amenities, don't you think?'

'And you didn't find out whether someone bought it?'

'I didn't want to know.'

'Why not?'

'I just didn't.' But, as her gaze was drawn back to her beloved lighthouse, she knew that wasn't enough of an answer. She'd never really thought about her reason herself but standing here was like being on a bridge to the past.

Old ground on one side. New ground on the other because Jake was there. The past and the future? For whatever reason, it felt important to say more.

'I guess it felt like it was ours. When Grandpa was the lighthouse keeper we knew the government owned it, but you couldn't put a face to anyone and they weren't going to change things and make it into a tourist resort or clear the bush for farming or something. It was ours. Part of our family. Where our roots were. If I knew it had been sold or—worse—the name of the person or people, it would stop being ours and I'd lose something precious. A part of my family when I'd already lost too much.'

Jake was nodding as if he understood, but he didn't say anything for a long time. He stood close beside her, looking up at the impressive height of the lighthouse. 'There's something magic about them, isn't there? Steeped in legends and with the history of dramatic shipwrecks swirling around the rocks they're guarding. Symbols of danger and safety at the same time.'

'Mmm...' A bit like Jake, then. How could she feel so safe in his company when she knew how dangerous it was to her heart?

The imaginary bridge beneath her feet was evaporating and the lines between her past and her future blurring, as if the magic of the lighthouse was drifting over her.

'Come with me.' She held out her hand. 'If the track hasn't disappeared, I can show you what used to be my favourite place.'

The track led down to the only point on the island where a boat could land, but they didn't need to go as far down as the dilapidated jetty. Halfway down the cliff you could still turn off and scramble to where massive boulders had shifted to form a kind of basin shape and pohutukawa trees grew almost sideways to provide shelter from the brisk sea breeze and dappled shade from a surprisingly hot autumn afternoon.

Directly under the lighthouse, they could see its shape through the canopy of leaves. Directly below them, waves crashed over more of the huge, volcanic boulders but the sound was muted, like the view of the lighthouse. This was a private spot in an already completely isolated place.

'This was where I always came when I was a kid,' Ellie said. 'When I wanted to be by myself.'

'You're not by yourself now.' Jake's eyes held a question.

'I'm where I want to be,' she said simply. Her heart was beating a tattoo inside her chest. 'With you.'

Jake dropped the basket and took a step closer to Ellie. Without taking his gaze from hers, he lifted his hand to touch her cheek and then cradled her chin as he tilted his head and brought his lips to hers.

Hints of the cool sea breeze kissed Ellie's skin as Jake

helped her out of her clothes. She could even taste the salt of it on Jake's skin as she got to kiss places she had only stolen a glimpse of before. She could still hear the sound of the waves below, but that sense faded, along with sight as her eyes drifted shut. Touch and taste were all that existed.

The touch of Jake's hands as he shaped her body as if imprinting it as quickly as possible on his memory cells. Learning the feel of her breasts and the silky skin of her inner thighs. She was doing the same thing. Too overwhelmed to do anything more than skate over what she wanted to learn so badly. The delicious dimples of his hardened nipples. The pulsing heat of his arousal. There would be time later for retracing these steps with the attention they deserved. Right now, a release from tension that had been building for far too long was what they both desperately needed.

And it was over too soon but they both knew it was only a beginning.

'Now we can take our time.' Jake smiled. 'We've got hours before our transport comes back.' His hand was still resting on her breast and the tiny circles he made with the tip of his little finger were enough to make her nipple hard again.

But Ellie wanted to touch, too. Turning on the blanket of the woollen Swanndri shirt Jake had insisted on wearing for the visit to Pēpe, she ran a fingertip down the intriguing tattoo.

'What does it say?'

'He who dares wins.'

Ellie liked that. She could use the mantra herself. And, in this moment, it seemed like a truth. She was daring here, allowing herself to fall in love again. To dream of a future. It even seemed possible that she could win Jake.

'And this?' Her fingertip had reached the end of the tattoo, just past the jut of hipbone. 'It's yin and yang, isn't it?'

'That's for being a twin. Ben has one too. He didn't go with the Chinese characters, though. Thought it was tacky thing to do.'

'I think it's beautiful.' Yin and yang. Two shapes that curved together to make a perfect circle. Two parts of a whole. Was that discordant jangle a hint of jealousy that it was his twin brother who was that close to Jake?

When *she* wanted to be?

Did something show on her face? Jake traced the outline of her cheek and jaw before pressing a soft kiss to her lips.

'You were wrong, you know.'

'What about?'

'About it being like having two of yourself, having a twin. We're very different. I don't think he even understands me. I'm not sure anyone does.'

Ellie's whisper felt like a promise. '*I'd* like to.'

His smile was a reward all by itself. 'I'd like you to.'

Ellie's fingers drifted sideways from where they'd been touching the symbol. She didn't want to talk about Jake's brother any more. This was *their* time. Hers and Jake's. Who knew when—or even if—they would ever get another time like this?

She felt Jake stir and harden beneath her hand and heard the way he caught his breath.

She was smiling as his mouth claimed hers again. Nobody else existed and this…this was paradise.

It was no surprise that there were reporters waiting to cover Jake's return to the camping ground, but he wasn't really prepared for it either. His heart sank as he saw the cameras. This wasn't good.

Maybe it had been a mistake to crack that bottle of champagne on the flight back from Half Moon Island.

More likely, it had been too hard to hide the glow that

their time together in the privacy of the island had left shining in their faces and the loose-limbed relaxation of their bodies. Laughter came too easily and it seemed physically impossible not to hold eye contact for a heartbeat longer than was socially acceptable if they were just friends. And he was still holding the hand he had taken to help Ellie alight from the helicopter.

He dropped it hastily. 'I'll deal with this,' he said. 'Just head off to your own cabin as though this afternoon never happened.'

Ellie managed a very creditable casual wave as she turned away before they got too close to the waiting photographers and she raised her voice so that her words could be clearly heard.

'Thanks, Jake. It's been fun. And I'll keep in touch about how Pēpe's doing.'

Nice try but Jake could sense the expectation ahead of him. These guys knew they were onto something.

'Had a nice afternoon, Jake?'

'Where did you take Ms Sutton?'

'You're looking happy, mate. You're not going to deny that there's something going on between you two, are you?'

Jake considered trying to silence the barrage of questions with a filthy look but he knew that would be tantamount to admitting he had something he wanted to hide. So, instead, he grinned at the cameras.

'No story here, sorry. I've been bird watching, that's all. And soaking up some of the stunning scenery this country's got to offer.'

'*With* Ellie Sutton.'

Jake's head shake was amused. Dismissive. 'Of course. She's got just as much of a vested interest in how our baby kiwi is doing as I have.'

'She's very different from your ex-wife, isn't she? Couldn't be more different.'

'Exactly.' Fear about Ellie running because of media interference in their lives was getting harder to contain. He had to put them off. 'Not my type, as you've so kindly pointed out. Yes, we visited the bird-rearing centre together. And, yes, we had lunch, but you're all wasting your time. It means absolutely nothing.'

His smile became more relaxed as he saw two reporters exchange disappointed looks. One had to have a last try.

'You were holding her hand.'

'As any gentleman would, helping a lady alight from a helicopter. Now, if you'll excuse me, I've got things to do. I'm sure you do, too. There's a lot that's going to be happening in the next day or two.'

'It's weather-dependent, isn't it? Shooting the shipwreck scene?'

'Yes. But I believe the forecast isn't too bad. Check the press release. Or talk to Kirsty. I'll talk to you again soon, yeah?'

Jake walked away, confident that he'd put them off the scent.

That he'd protected Ellie, at least for now.

But it wouldn't last, would it? At some point, if he wanted to keep Ellie in his life, it would have to be made public.

Jake had no idea what would happen then.

What he did have a very clear idea of, however, was that he *did* absolutely want to keep Ellie in his life.

And it was looking more and more like he might want that for ever.

The weather wasn't as good as expected over the next couple of days and the sea swell was too big to make filming close to shore safe. Camera crews were dispatched to get some good footage of the wild surf at Cathedral Cove that could be used later and there was some editing work, production meetings and rehearsals going on that Jake was involved with, but there wasn't much for Ellie to do.

She tried to use her time productively and got out her laptop to work on some of the lecture material she was writing on aeromedical transportation, but the world of academia and even front-line rescue work seemed very distant. It wasn't long before she was checking in with the local meteorological website for both the short-and long-range weather forecasts. She almost hoped the weather would stay uncooperative because when the final scenes had been done, this interlude in her life would be over, and what would happen then between her and Jake?

He'd go back to the United States. Move on to his next movie project.

Email for a while, perhaps. Talk on the phone occasionally?

And then the contact would fade and all she'd have left would be memories of time spent with the most remarkable man she'd ever met.

Finding herself doodling a yin and yang design in her notebook made Ellie sigh and drop her pen. She clicked out of the page of weather charts and found herself on the home page of the news service she favoured. The pop-up box of hot topics was one she never normally took any notice of, but Jake's name jumped out, along with the words '...denies new romance...'

It only took a tiny movement of her hand to click on the link and there it was—a photograph of her and Jake with their hands linked, laughing as they ducked and ran from the private helicopter.

Looking, for all the world, like a couple in love.

*Jacob Logan categorically denies any love interest with the mysterious paramedic who's not dishing on the time she shared with the star recently in the wake of rescuing him so dramatically. Could it be that he's protesting too much? Judge for yourself.*

The triangular 'play' button on the video clip was also only a click away. And there was Jake, smiling confidently.

*'...not my type, as you've so kindly pointed out. Yes, we visited the bird-rearing centre together. And, yes, we had lunch, but you're all wasting your time. It means absolutely nothing.'*

How believable was that dismissive tone? That amused smile that said they were all barking up a totally ridiculous tree?

It wasn't true. He was just saying that to protect her from the media. To keep what they had private. But, even knowing that, it was still so...convincing. And weren't the best lies the ones that were a version of the truth?

Echoes of things that had unwillingly embedded themselves in her brain floated to the surface. Like what the camp manager had said. *It's not as if anything lasts in Tinseltown...*

And Jill—her most trusted friend—had had her doubts, hadn't she? *Be careful...I don't want you getting hurt again...*

The echoes became a chant until a new thought rocked Ellie. They'd been so careful to keep things secret, but was that really because it was something special and private? Or was it because it actually wasn't important? Because it meant absolutely *nothing*?

Stunned, Ellie slowly closed the lid of her laptop. She sat there, in her cabin, for a long, long time, trying to make sense of the emotional roller-coaster she'd been on ever since she'd met Jake.

She'd believed in the connection they'd made at the start, only to have it dismissed with the distant way Jake had treated her at that first press conference.

She'd totally believed him during that heartfelt conversation on the beach and…yes, she'd been insanely flattered that he'd pretended he'd been kissing her instead of Amber when he'd filmed that *perfect* scene.

Jake could never know how much it had meant to tell him that she trusted him, and that *had* been the truth.

Or had she been acting herself without realising it? Trying on that new skin that would allow her to be the best person she could be? It had felt so good, too.

She'd willingly gone along with the game of ramping up the sexual tension, but now she'd swooped down to a new low on the roller-coaster and the skin was too tight.

It felt like it was ripping in places.

Bleeding.

What if this was all just a game to someone who could make people believe whatever he wanted to make them believe?

And she was just as gullible as she'd always been?

# CHAPTER TEN

HE HADN'T SEEN Ellie for hours.

When the afternoon wore on into the evening, everybody gathered for a meal. Standing beside Steve as they joined the queue to help themselves to steak and salad, Jake took another look around.

'Seen Ellie today?'

Steve shook his head. 'Things were quiet. She said she needed some time to work on lecture notes or something. She's probably in her cabin.'

'Might let her know it's time for dinner.' Jake abandoned his empty plate and slipped away.

Something about how quiet this part of the camping ground was made Jake frown. Or maybe it was the closed look of the cabin he knew was Ellie's. The door was shut. The curtains on the small window were drawn. He knocked on the door with a sense of foreboding that only increased sharply when he saw her face.

'What's wrong?'

'Nothing.' Her voice was tight. '*Absolutely* nothing, in fact.'

Good grief…had she been *crying?*

'Ellie…' Jake gave the door a push, but Ellie was pushing back, keeping it only slightly ajar.

She was clearly upset about something. Her words, and

their tone, repeated themselves in his head. *Absolutely* nothing.

Oh, no… Had someone printed what he'd said in dismissing any suspicion of their relationship? Had she *believed* it? How could she? It was too ridiculous for words.

'Let me in.' It was a command, not a request, and Jake emphasised his intent by a shove at the door that Ellie couldn't prevent.

'Someone might see you.'

'I couldn't give a damn.' Jake pushed the door shut behind him with his foot. 'We need to talk. This is about what I said to those reporters about our day together, isn't it?'

She didn't say anything. She didn't need to.

'You *believed* it?'

That hurt, dammit.

'I didn't want to believe it.' The rawness in Ellie's voice only added to his own hurt. 'It was the *last* thing I wanted to believe but you're *so* good at lying.'

'Acting.' The word was a defensive snap. 'For both our sakes. You should have known that's what I was doing. I thought—*hoped*—you knew me better than that. That you would know I was trying to protect you.'

'By *lying*?'

He couldn't win, could he? The pain of being labelled a liar and untrustworthy was gathering heat and morphing into anger.

'What did you want me to say, Ellie? That I'd just had the most incredible afternoon of my life, making love to the woman I'm head over heels in love with?'

Her jaw dropped and she went a shade paler. No wonder. He was almost shouting, which wasn't exactly a romantic way to tell someone how you felt about them, but he had to try and make her understand.

'Can you imagine what that would have unleashed?

Do you want the whole world pointing out how different our lives are? What the odds are that it could never
work? Dredging up all the sordid drama of my last marriage? Finding people they could pay to reveal details of
your past?'

Yes. She was beginning to understand. He could see the
flicker of fear in her eyes. His voice softened.

'I know you have things you'd rather keep hidden and
I respect that. I'm not going to ask you what they are because I know you'll tell me when you're ready to. When
you trust me enough.'

'I *want* to trust you, Jake. I do…but…'

Her voice trailed into silence but she wanted to believe
him and maybe that was enough. All he needed to do was
chase the last of that uncertainty from her eyes. What he
said next might be the most important lines of his life.

'I want that day to have a chance to get here,' he said
slowly. 'I want…'

What did he want?

So much. A future that included Ellie. The longing was
so fierce that it made the prospect of failure terrifying.

Words deserted Jake. This was too big to try and put
into words because he might get it wrong. What could he
say that might help Ellie see the same future he could?

Future…

Suddenly the words were there. Jake swallowed hard
and stepped closer to Ellie without breaking their eye contact by so much as a blink.

'I can see the future in your eyes,' he said softly. '*My*
future. Without you, it's not going to happen and…and you
can't begin to know how much that scares me…'

There was more he should say but the words vanished
as swiftly as they had come. He'd hit a kind of verbal wall
and it felt jarring. Had he said the wrong thing?

No. From the way Ellie's gaze was softening, his words had hit the right note. He could close the gap between them now and kiss her and everything would be okay.

Except that Ellie shifted her head back a fraction. Enough to stop his movement.

'You don't need to lie to protect me, Jake,' she said. 'I can look after myself. And—if this *is* real, it can't stay hidden for ever, can it?'

'No.' Jake touched her lips softly with his own. 'And I don't want it to. But let's just get through the next few days and get this filming finished before the world goes crazy.'

The next kiss made it feel like it should. Made Jake feel like they were back on Half Moon Island and the whole world was right there in his arms.

'Does anyone know where you are?'

'Only Steve. He won't say anything.'

'So you could stay for a while?'

'Oh, yeah…' It was becoming such a familiar pleasure, scooping Ellie into his arms and taking her somewhere.

And taking her to bed was the best possible place.

Cathedral Cove was a perfect location for what would be the most dramatic scenes of this movie. The marine reserve area was only accessible by boat or on foot, which led to some major logistical issues for the huge crew, but the setting was a jewel in a country already renowned for its unbeatable scenery. With a backdrop of sheer limestone cliffs topped with ancient pohutukawa trees, the cove was named for the spectacular archway rock formation that linked its two beaches.

The frame of the archway, with the sinking ship in the sea beyond would be used for the scene in which Jake saved Amber's life and ensured that history would stay the same. First he had to persuade her to jump off the ship, keep her afloat in the waves despite the dead weight of her long dress and petticoats and then carry her through the surf and onto the safety of the beach.

Everybody was hoping a single take would be enough, especially Ellie, who'd had to carry all the gear she might need to the scene in a backpack. There were rescue boats available and she had lots of foil blankets in case of hypothermia but it was going to be a long and tense day.

No amount of anxiety or tension could undermine how happy she felt, though. Jake had told her he was in love with her—albeit in a roundabout way—with what he could have told those reporters. The time he'd spent with her last night had told her more than any words could anyway, and soon—when these final scenes were in the can—he would stop trying to hide anything and then she could really trust that this was, in fact, *real*. That she and Jake had a future together.

Her heart was in her mouth as she watched Jake jump from the tilted ship. Why wasn't he using a stunt double, like Amber was? Boats stayed near enough to help if needed during the difficult swim and then they had to reposition everyone to do the bit where an exhausted Jake staggered through the shallower surf to carry the heroine to safety.

Just like he'd carried her when they'd still been strangers.

She could remember the comfort of being encircled by those strong arms and being carried to safety. She'd thought later how amazing it would be to be able to trust someone as protective and caring as Jake.

And she was so nearly there. As scary as it was, she was ready to trust him completely with her heart. With her life. To banish for ever those warning whispers in the back of her mind.

She was close enough to hear every word of the final beach scene to be filmed. To be so proud of Jake as he played his role to perfection—using modern medical resuscitation procedures to save the life of someone who would have died if this had really been back in the eighteenth century.

The portal that would take him back to the present day was within the ancient stone archway and the heart-wrenching scene where Jake had to leave the woman he thought he loved but could never be with was gripping.

Especially that last kiss.

Was he still pretending that Amber was *her?* Ellie was having trouble hiding a tender smile as she watched. And listened. She could certainly pretend that she was the one being kissed and, yes…it did make her feel uncomfortable, watching Jake kiss another woman, but she'd have to get used to this, wouldn't she? She had to remind herself that he was only acting here. When he was with her, it was *real*.

Jake was holding Amber in his arms now. The cameras moved in for a close-up.

'I can see the future in your eyes,' he said softly. '*My* future. Without you, it's not going to happen and…and you can't begin to know how much that scares me…'

The smile on Ellie's lips died. Those words he'd said to her that had finally won her fragile trust had been nothing more than lines in a script, written by someone else. A rehearsal for an upcoming scene.

She felt faint. Dizzy and sick.

A huge cheer went up from cast and crew as the director signalled that this was a wrap and filming was over. Even if she'd wanted to, she couldn't have got near Jake in the midst of the congratulatory buzz and the chaos of moving all the people and gear from this location.

But that was fine.

Because she *didn't* want to get near him. Not before she'd got her head around this. Before she knew how on earth she was going to handle what felt like a kind of death.

There was nothing like the buzz of a wrap party.

The hard work was over, at least for the cast and crew. There was still a lot to do, of course, and Jake would be very busy for the next few weeks because he wanted to be involved with the post-production work. Thank goodness Steve had contracted some brilliant New Zealand musicians to write and record the score, and this country was beginning to lead the world in special effects. It gave him a reason to stay here for some time. Enough time, hopefully, for he and Ellie to figure out how they were going to make things work. To nurture their newborn love and make it strong enough to withstand the pressures that would inevitably come.

Jake's heart sank when he saw Ellie finally arrive but stay on the outskirts of the exuberant gathering. She looked tired and less than happy despite the smiles with which she was greeting the people she'd come to know. She wasn't enjoying being with them and that was a worry. These people were his colleagues. The faces might change from movie to movie, but the feeling of camaraderie was always the same. By the time they got to the end of a big production like this, having coped with all the hassles and hiccups, there was a real sense of being comrades-in-arms. A family.

It took a while for him for fight his way to where Ellie was standing.

'It's over, babe. Real life can resume.' He couldn't wipe the grin off his face. 'As soon as we're back in Auckland, I'm heading straight for the barber shop. You won't know me.'

'Yeah…' Ellie's smile looked brittle. 'It *is* over.'

Someone thumped Jake on the shoulder as they went past. 'Well done, Doctor.' They laughed. 'Another life saved.'

Jake ignored them. He was staring at Ellie, trying to make the connection that should automatically be there when he looked into her eyes.

But it wasn't. It was like shutters were down and there was no way he could see past them.

'I'm all packed,' Ellie said. 'I'm heading home as soon as I've said goodbye to everyone.'

Jake simply stared. Bewildered. Demanding an explanation for the inexplicable. Why was Ellie raining on his parade like this? Okay, they'd hit a speed bump yesterday but they'd sorted all that last night, hadn't they?

More than sorted it, as far as he'd been aware.

'I thought you'd been honest with me last night.' Ellie's voice was dangerously quiet. 'I actually believed what you said about the future, but you were just practising your lines, weren't you? "*I can see the future in your eyes.*"' The mimicking of his voice was painful. '"*My future.*"'

Oh…*God*… He *had* used those lines. Because he'd been lost for words and that bit of his script in the back of his head had happened to be just what he'd wanted to say. No wonder the words had come so easily. Why hadn't he realised why they'd suddenly jarred?

He must have looked as horrified as he was feeling. The look Ellie gave him dripped with pity.

'You didn't even notice, did you? I don't think you even know the difference between reality and fiction. It's all fake, isn't it?'

'*No…*' But Jake could hear echoes of the accusations Ben had levelled at him so many times.

'Do *you* even know who *you* really are, Jake Logan?'

'Of course I do. And so do you. You know me better than anyone, Ellie. You know more about who I am now than even Ben does.'

His tone was fierce enough for someone approaching them to take a second glance and turn away hurriedly.

'But I can't *trust* you.' The words were clearly being torn from a painful place.

'Don't do this.' Jake cast a desperate look over his shoulder. How could the party be still going in full swing when the bottom was falling out of his world? He had no idea how he could fix this.

*If* he could fix it.

And a tiny voice in the back of his head was asking him if he even wanted to if it was going to be this difficult.

'You said I'd tell you what I'd been hiding when I was ready to. Well…I'm ready.'

'When you trusted me enough, I said.'

'What comes first, do you think? Trust…or love?' Ellie didn't wait for an answer. 'I grew up with my parents and my grandfather—people I loved with all my heart and trusted without ever having to question it.'

He could see the muscles move in her throat as she swallowed hard. 'When you lose someone you love that much you lose a part of your soul and I…I lost everyone I had.'

He wanted to touch Ellie. To try and comfort her. To let her know that she still had someone. *Him*. But Jake knew that she wouldn't welcome the touch. She had more she wanted to say.

'It took a long, long time before I was ready to risk that kind of pain again. To love again. But I finally did. I met Michael and I fell in love. We dated for about two years and when he asked me to marry him, I was happy to say yes.'

Her tone was almost conversational. 'I already had the house with the picket fence but I was so ready for the husband who would be the father of my babies. The wedding was all planned. He travelled a lot with his consultancy work, but he promised me that we'd make it work. I just had to trust him.'

Jake knew this story was not going to end well. The sinking feeling he'd had when he'd first seen Ellie this evening was getting rapidly stronger.

She had an odd smile curling her lips now. There was no hint of genuine amusement in it.

'I guess I'm lucky that his wife and three kids didn't turn up at the church in that bit where they ask if anyone knows any reason why someone can't be lawfully wed. He left his phone behind one day when he went out to the shops to get some milk and for some reason I picked it up and answered it when it rang. His wife thought I was a colleague who was attending some conference with him. She asked me to pass on the message that he needed to remember to pick up the birthday cake for their daughter on his way home.'

Jake was stunned. 'He wasn't really going to go through with a bigamous marriage, was he?'

Ellie shrugged. 'That's not the point, is it, Jake? The point is that I trusted him. Believed everything he told me. I'm willing to bet that his wife believed everything he told her, too—all the lies that covered the time he spent with me.' She turned her head enough to break their eye contact. 'I loved him and I trusted him and when I lost him I realised I'd lost another part of me. On top of all the other parts I'd already lost. And I knew there wasn't enough of me left to risk that again because if I lost any more there might be nothing left.'

He could see the slow tears tracing the side of her nose and the tremble in her voice was heartbreaking. 'I knew I'd never be able to trust another man like that, but then

I went and fell in love with you. Of all the people in the world, I had to pick an award-winning actor.'

She looked back and Jake had never seen so much pain in anyone's eyes. He couldn't hope to make this better. It was too big.

But he had to try.

'So you're going to throw away what we've found together? Because I made the stupid mistake of saying something that was in my head thanks to a script? Because I couldn't think of a better way to say it myself?'

That tiny voice in his head was there again. Man, she's got issues, it said, but it's not your job to try and fix her. Maybe nobody can. And if she's prepared to throw it away this easily it can't mean that much to her anyway.

'What we had wasn't real. Any more than my "engagement" was real. It's all a fantasy. You're watching yourself on a big screen all the time, Jake—whether you're aware of it or not. It's the way you live your life, but I can't live like that. I don't have a script and I don't want one.'

Not being able to help soothe the pain of someone he cared about this much felt like an epic failure. Jake wasn't up to the task and it made him feel inadequate. As useless at keeping a woman happy as—God help him—his father had been?

What had he done that was *so* wrong? All he'd tried to do was love Ellie. And keep her safe. She wasn't the only one with trust issues and wasn't she doing pretty much what she thought he'd done to her? Offering something precious, only to snatch it away again?

This wasn't fair, but it *was* happening and now fear kicked in. He was going to lose Ellie and there was no way this scene could end well.

Fear and frustration were easy to twist into anger, but was he going to harness that anger to fight for this? For *them?*

'I can never, ever know whether you're for real or whether you're acting because I've been there before. Michael may not have been a famous actor, but he was as good at pretending as you are.' She seemed to get taller as she straightened her spine. 'I can't ever trust you and without trust there's nothing. Nothing worth fighting for anyway.'

She wasn't going to fight, then. So why should he?

'You're right,' she said softly. 'It's over. *Really* over.'

This time, when she turned her head, she began to walk away as well. But she had one last parting shot to send over her shoulder.

'Reality isn't that bad, Jake. Maybe you could try it one day.'

# CHAPTER ELEVEN

*Nothing worth fighting for.*

The words were a mantra now. Part of him agreed wholeheartedly. The part that wanted to argue just needed to be reminded that it took two to tango and if one of them didn't think it was worth fighting for, it was pointless for the other to batter themselves to bits in the name of a hopeless cause.

There were elements of drama queen in it as well that reminded Jake disturbingly of his mother's reaction to life. Blowing things out of proportion. Overreacting. Making grand gestures. Did her suicide have anything to do with trying to turn real life into a scripted drama? A grand gesture gone wrong?

Maybe he'd finally find out.

Ben was unexpectedly in the country and they'd arranged to meet in Auckland after Jake's busy day of setting up the post-production work he was really looking forward to.

*Had* been looking forward to, anyway.

The creativity that came with the editing and sound and special effects were more satisfying than acting in many ways. Jake had been seeing his future moving in this direction for a while now and he'd viewed the next few weeks as the highlight of this whole project.

Even more so, given that it would have provided extra time with Ellie.

But Ellie was gone and her cutting last words had fuelled an anger that he was trying to hang onto because it made her disappearance from his life easier to handle.

Or not.

He couldn't keep her out of his head. No matter how hard he tried to concentrate, it seemed like every few minutes something would sift through a tiny gap in the barrier. Images of her face—the way it changed and softened with that special smile that he knew was only for him. The tone of her voice—and her laughter. The way the connection between them had made him feel…like that moment they'd looked at each other when Pēpe had been hatching.

Even Steve noticed that he wasn't entirely present in some of those meetings.

'You don't like the music?'

'I love it.'

'Could've fooled me. And the workshop for special effects? It's going to be fantastic, don't you think?'

'Absolutely.'

Steve just gave him a look. Shook his head and moved off to talk with the crowd of technical wizards they were pulling together.

No wonder he wasn't in the best of moods when he walked down to the bar he'd heard of near the Viaduct to meet Ben. It was late. He was tired.

Tired of the silent battle going on in his head.

And his heart.

He missed Ellie…

She was no drama queen like his mother. You couldn't get more real than Ellie. She didn't have a script and she didn't want one.

She thought he was fake. And here he was about to spend time with his brother, who also thought he was fake.

It was important to see him, though. If there was some way they could resolve the lingering tension between them, at least he'd have someone back in his life who meant the world to him.

He wouldn't continue feeling so...so *lonely*.

It had been weeks since the brothers had seen each other and initially it was too much like a rerun of their reunion after the rescue. Huge relief at seeing the other was okay but there was an undercurrent that was swirling over rocks that weren't very far below the surface. Weird to feel nervous about talking to Ben but Jake felt his heart skip a beat as the small talk faded. Jake needed to find a way to steer the conversation towards what really mattered.

'I gather you're not here just to see me?'

'That's why I'm here in Auckland.'

'That's not what I meant. Why come to New Zealand?'

'I brought Mary home.'

'Mary?'

'The girl who saved my life. She came to New York, but she was ill so I brought her home.'

The words were stark. The sentences bald enough for Jake to know there was a lot being left unsaid. But they were still too far apart. He needed to tread carefully if he wanted to get as close as they had once been. Close enough to really talk about the biggest rock in that undercurrent?

'So now you're heading back?'

'Yes. Tomorrow.'

'How ill is she?'

'She's okay now.'

'And you're not getting involved any further?'

'I brought her home. In the company jet.'

Jake couldn't suppress a soft snort. He knew what was happening here. The control Ben was trying to exert over himself. That he was trying to protect himself. Surely it was enough that one of them was dealing with the dark side of emotional involvement with a woman right now. Maybe Ben needed a push to wake up and smell the roses before it was too late for both of them.

'That's involvement?' The words came out more harshly than he'd intended.

'Cut it with the snide, Jake.'

'I'm not snide,' he said, on an inward sigh. 'I'm worried.'

'She'll be fine.'

'I'm worried about you.'

'Why on earth…?' He could see the way Ben's eyes widened. *He* was the big brother. He was the one who got to be worried.

'I've met a woman, too, Ben,' he said. 'Same as you, it's the woman who plucked me out of the sea. Only, unlike you, I'm in it up to my neck and…well, it's not going so well right about now.'

Talk about an understatement. Why had he said that anyway? It wasn't 'not going so well'. It was *over*. And he didn't even want to try and fight that decision.

Or maybe he did. Maybe even sorting things out with his brother wasn't going to make that lonely place disappear. Man…this was confusing. And how could he begin to try and explain that to Ben when his brother's expression suggested that he couldn't be bothered with another one of Jake's dramas. He even held up a hand as if to ward off any more information.

'You don't need to tell me. Of course it's not going well. But there's no need to talk about it—I'll be reading about it in the glossies soon enough. Maybe it's time you grew up, Jake. Marriages and happy endings belong in one of your movies. They're not the real world. Not for us, that's for sure. You've already tried and failed. You play-acted the perfect husband last time. Wasn't that enough?'

Ben was angry. Fed up with him, or was there something else bothering him even more? Jake was pretty sure there was more to this reaction than the embarrassing publicity that had come in the wake of his failed celebrity marriage. Had he really believed he was in love then? Had Ben been able to see something he hadn't?

'You think I was acting?'

'You've acted all your life—just like our mother. You don't know what's real and what's not.'

And there was Ellie's voice in his head yet again.

*You're watching yourself on a big screen all the time, Jake—whether you're aware of it or not.*

It wasn't true.

'I wasn't acting the first time round,' he told Ben. It was the truth. He'd believed he'd been in love, but he hadn't really known the meaning of the word, had he? 'Believe it or not, I thought it was real. But now…I'm sure not acting this time. Ellie's different. She's one in a million. This is a million miles from one failed marriage.'

Ben looked really angry now. He jerked himself to his feet. 'Then you're even more of a fool than I thought. One in a million—just like the last one. And the next one and the one after that?'

The sarcasm in his brother's tone was enough to push Jake's buttons. He didn't know Ellie. He had no idea that he was dismissing the most amazing woman on the planet. He pushed himself to his feet, his fists clenched.

'Will you cut it out?' They were getting noticed. The bar might be empty of punters but the barman was watching them carefully. 'Ellie *is* different, Ben. And we're not... we're not our parents, Ben.'

'What's that supposed to mean?'

'Just that. We're our own people.' Jake took a deep breath. 'You finally let it out, didn't you? In the life raft when you said I wouldn't know reality if it bit me. That I was just like Mom. You told me she'd killed herself and you think I'm on the same path. Heading for self-destruction because I can't pick what's real or deal with it.'

'I don't...' Ben's face was agonised. He couldn't find the words.

'Yeah, you do. It's gutted me knowing that Mom's death was suicide, but it's gutted me even more that you've kept it to yourself all these years. You've been protecting me, but you didn't have to. You've been protecting yourself and that's even worse.'

Ben shook his head. 'This isn't making any sense.'

'Maybe it's not.' Jake wasn't sure of what he was trying to say either, but the words kept spilling out. 'But this girl you brought all the way to New Zealand. Mary. She went all the way to the States to see *you?*'

'So...what?'

'I'm not even beginning to guess what that was all about,' Jake continued, 'but I don't have to guess because it doesn't make any difference. No matter who she is, no matter what she's done, no matter what she means to you, you'll never open yourself up. Because if you do, you'll have to open yourself up to the whole mess that was our mom. Our family. And Mom killed herself. Finally, I'm seeing why you're so damned afraid.'

'I'm not afraid.' A knee-jerk response. Defensive.

'If you're not afraid of relationships, then why assume that whatever I have going on with Ellie will inevitably be another disaster for the glossies to gloat over?' He turned away. 'Well, maybe it is a disaster, but at least I'm involved. I know I'm capable of loving. I'm not running away, like you.'

'Oh, for...' Ben was barely controlling his anger now. 'I'm not *running away* from anything.'

'It looks that way to me. You run. You hide. Just like you've been hiding from me all these years by not telling me the truth. Shall we go there, Ben? Talk about it properly? Or do you want to run away from that, too?'

Despair and anger were a curdled mess in his gut. Things were going so wrong here and he couldn't stop it. They were standing here in this deserted bar and staring at each other. If they'd still been ten years old one of them would have thrown a punch by now. Or twenty years old.

Maybe they still would.

The moment could have gone either way, but Jake could see so many things in Ben's face. Fear that what he was saying might be true? Sadness that they were so far apart? A willingness to try and put things right?

It wasn't going to happen, though. Not yet.

'I need to go.' Ben's tone was final.

'Of course you do.' Jake's anger was draining away, leaving a horrible empty feeling in his gut. 'People talk about emotions, you run. You've spent our lives accusing me of being like Mom every time I showed emotion. Play-acting. Yeah, okay...maybe some of it was, but not all of it. I'm trying to figure it out at last. Maybe the real is worth fighting for. The real is even worth hurting for.'

It sounded good to say it out loud.

Right.

'Yeah, well, good luck with that.' It was Ben who was being snide this time. 'What did you say—that things aren't going well between you and this new woman? Amazing. I stand amazed.'

'Get out of here before I slug you,' Jake snapped. He didn't need Ben echoing the other voice in his head. The one that was trying to persuade him to let it go. To let Ellie go. That it *wasn't* worth fighting for.

As if on cue, Ben's phone started ringing.

Someone wanted to talk to Ben. Mary?

What if it had been Ellie ringing *him* right now? Would he want to answer it?

The strength of his affirmation went a long way towards sorting his current confusion.

'Maybe you should get that,' he growled. 'Maybe it's Mary.'

'It's work.' But Ben clearly wanted to answer the call.

'There you go, then.' Jake turned away. 'I don't know why you're not taking it. Work's always been your place to hide, hasn't it, big brother? Why should anything I say make it any different?'

Well…

That had gone well.

*Not.*

He'd had a few beers with Ben in the bar, but that was a long time ago now. Needing to burn off some of the anger and frustration, Jake had taken a long route back to his hotel to try to walk it off.

All he'd succeeded in burning off had been any mellowing effect the beers might have had. Maybe he needed something stronger. Just as well the minibar in his room was well stocked.

The first Scotch didn't even touch sides. He could, at least, taste the second. The third ended up sitting in its glass on the coffee table in front of him as Jake tipped his head back with a groan of frustration. He went to push his hair back but the barber had dealt with the long locks today and there were no tangles to provide the welcome distraction of pain. He rubbed at his chin. Clean shaven now. He'd been looking forward to getting rid of that beard.

Looking forward to finding out what it would feel like to kiss Ellie without it. Hoping she'd love the change and be attracted to him all over again with that same passion they'd discovered between them.

Maybe he did need that third Scotch after all.

What was going so wrong in his life?

He'd lost Ellie.

It felt like he might have really lost Ben this time, too.

Sleep wasn't an option but sitting here for hour after hour, trying to make sense of the downward spiral his personal life was taking, wasn't either. By 2:00 a.m. he'd had enough. He punched in the number of Ben's phone, only to get an engaged signal. Who was he talking to at 2:00 a.m.?

This Mary maybe?

More likely to be someone in New York.

Whatever. Jake dropped the phone and closed his eyes. If he didn't catch at least a few hours' sleep, he'd have trouble keeping up with the hectic schedule tomorrow would bring. And if he couldn't keep up with the play, he might as well kiss goodbye any ambitions he had to move into a directing and editing role in the near future.

Things were bad enough already. He really couldn't afford to let his life spin any more out of control right now.

'I wish I could help, hon. I hate seeing you so sad.'

'It's helping being here, Jill. I love this place.'

Ellie was spending the afternoon at the bird-rearing centre. There was always plenty for a knowledgeable volunteer to do. The brooder pens needed to be wiped down and the peat moss dug over and checked for moisture content. Food for the older chicks needed preparation by mincing the beef heart to mix with shredded fruit and vegetables. If she was lucky, she would get to help weigh chicks or to sit quietly to observe and record their behaviour. A real treat would be helping to feed a chick, but there weren't any that needed that kind of assistance today. Maybe next time.

It *was* helping. Being here and being with one of her closest friends.

'How's the lecture writing going?'

'Okay, I guess.' Ellie put gloves on to push raw meat through the mincer. 'I've just finished one on the physiological effects of altitude. Tomorrow I'll get stuck into the biodynamics of flight. And I'm spending some time on base, getting images of aeromedical equipment. I'm keeping busy.'

'Are you enjoying it?'

'Honestly?' Ellie looked up as she moved to get a set of scales to start weighing portions of the minced beef. 'I don't think I'm cut out for an academic life. It's kind of lonely…and boring.'

'It'll be better when you're actually teaching it instead of writing about it.'

'Maybe.' Ellie was really trying hard to be optimistic but being less than honest with someone she trusted felt wrong. 'I'm not sure I'm cut out for being in a classroom, day in, day out, either. You know what they say? Those that can—do, those that can't—teach…'

'Nonsense.' Jillian emphasised her contradiction by turning on the food processor to shred some carrots. She threw Ellie a speculative glance when she turned it off again.

'Can you really not go back to active duty? Your ankle's fine now, isn't it?'

'My back isn't. That injury I had years ago was always going to limit my time on the choppers. It's time to be careful if I want to be walking properly when I'm old and gray.'

'You miss it, don't you?'

'Yeah…' But active duty as a paramedic wasn't the only thing Ellie was missing. Not by a long shot.

'You could go back on the road, then.'

Ellie shook her head. 'If I want to stay in the ambulance service, I'll either have to teach or I'll get put behind a desk as some kind of manager.' The dismal prospect made her throat feel tight. Or maybe that was due to the never-ending ache of what else she was missing.

*Jake…*

She tried to smile at Jillian. 'Maybe I'll just come and work for you instead.'

'Cool. We won't be able to pay you, but you'd be most welcome.'

Turning on the taps to wash some feeding bowls, Ellie had to blink hard. She needed to get over herself. There must be dozens of people who'd love the chance to do the kind of work she had the skills to do now. Like teach… or manage.

The problem was, she'd had a taste of things that were so much more exciting. Even if she knew she was lucky to have had that taste and there was no way to have it again, there was no easy way back to reality.

In her working life *or* her love life.

Jillian handed her one of the feed bowls when everything had been weighed and charted. 'That's Pēpe's. You get to feed him. He's your baby.'

The squeeze around Ellie's heart was a physical pain. He wasn't just hers, he was Jake's too. She'd never again be able to look at as much as a picture of a kiwi without thinking of him. Without the pain of knowing that she'd lost something precious. Not really fair when she lived in a country that had made the bird its national icon.

Except she hadn't lost it, had she?

It had never really been there. Just an illusion on her part and play-acting on Jake's.

If it had been real, she would have heard from him by now. How many days would it take before she gave up and started getting over him?

Right now it felt like there wouldn't be enough days in the rest of her life for that to happen.

She needed to try harder.

'Have you had any luck getting through the red tape for Pēpe's release? Did you find out who owns Half Moon Island now?'

'I'm working on it.' Jillian tapped the side of her nose. 'I have contacts. Give me a bit more time and I'll get it sorted.'

Ellie nodded. She managed a genuine smile this time.

A bit more time. Perhaps that *was* all that was needed. For Pēpe's release and for her own return to happiness.


The headache Jake had the next morning was entirely self-inflicted. The weariness was bone deep, but at least the combination of physical and emotional suffering made him feel like he might have finally hit rock bottom.

Did that mean the only way might be up?

It was during a meeting with sound technology experts that a moment of clarity hit. He wasn't the only person present who was dubious about what was being planned to emphasise the crashing of surf against rocks during the shipwreck scene and the music that would accompany it.

Steve was frowning. 'Isn't it a bit over the top?'

'It'll work,' the sound guy said. 'Trust us.'

And there was Ellie's voice in his head yet again.

*Without trust there's nothing.*

The echo stayed with Jake for the rest of the day. It got louder when he didn't have to focus on work and was trying to kill the last of his headache and fatigue with a brutal workout in the hotel gymnasium.

Lack of trust was what had blown them apart.

It was what was still wrong between himself and Ben.

With a towel knotted loosely around his hips, Jake caught his reflection in the locker-room mirrors as he walked back from the showers. His tattoo was such a part of his body these days he barely registered its presence unless it had to be masked for a scene. Or when someone asked about it. Like Ellie had.

It was actually possible to still feel the light touch of her fingers as she'd traced the characters. To hear his own voice as he'd explained their meaning.

*He who dares wins.*

Jake's step slowed. His gaze lifted to stare into his own eyes.

Did he dare?

Could he win what he wanted most?

The answer was suddenly crystal clear. He had no other choice but to try his best, because if he didn't, he would be haunted by what-ifs for the rest of his life.

But how?

Again, the answer seemed obvious. He would ask someone who might know. Someone whose advice he could trust.

This time, Ben answered his phone straight away. 'Jake… Hey, man! I'm glad you rang. I—'

'I need help,' Jake interrupted. He couldn't afford the distraction of any small talk. This was too important. 'I've done something and I don't know how to fix it. How to get Ellie to trust me again.'

She had every reason not to trust him. He'd proclaimed publicly that their relationship meant absolutely nothing and then he'd compounded the situation by using lines that had meant nothing because they were no more than part of a rehearsed script.

The silence on the other end of the line was startled. Jake rushed to fill it.

'I lied, Ben. I told the media that Ellie meant nothing to me.'

'Well…of course you did. They would have destroyed any privacy you could have had for the foreseeable future. You were protecting her.'

'That's what I thought. But what it's really done is destroy the trust that was there. And that's what matters most, isn't it? It's what's gone wrong between us, too.'

The silence was heavier this time. He could imagine Ben closing his eyes or starting to pace as he tried to figure out what to say to that.

'I understand that's why you lied about Mom,' Jake said quietly. 'To protect *me*. And it's okay. I *get* that and…and I still love you, man. It's why I knew you'd understand. Why you can help me out here.'

'It's not that simple.' The words were almost a sigh. 'I wasn't lying to protect you. I was trying to protect myself, I guess. I was…hiding—like you accused me of doing—and…I can't do that any more. I've…' He sounded choked now. 'I've learned something today. Something *huge*… and—'

Again Jake interrupted his brother. 'I don't understand. How were you trying to protect yourself?'

He didn't try and fill the silence this time. He simply waited it out.

'It was my fault.'

The incredulous huff came out almost like a snort of laughter. 'Are you *kidding* me?'

'You weren't there, Jake. You were in hospital, remember? And I was in jail for the night.'

'The car conversion incident. Of course I remember.' Jake couldn't help a wry smile. 'A highlight in the disreputable adolescence of the wild Logan boys.'

'Things were bad at home when I got out. Mom had a black eye and she was hysterical. She kept crying. Telling me how sorry she was. Telling me I had to look after you.'

'Sounds like Mom.' That sadness was never going to go away completely. Jake sighed. 'Was Dad responsible for the black eye or did she get drunk and fall over?'

'I'm pretty sure it was Dad.'

*'Bastard.'*

'You said it.'

'Even so, Mom was being a drama queen. That's the way she always reacted to stuff.'

'No. She was telling me she was going to kill herself. I could have done something, Jake, and I didn't. And I was too ashamed to tell anyone. That's why the coroner ruled it had been an accidental overdose. Because I was hiding and not telling the truth.

The expletive Jake used dismissed any credence the statement had.

'You were *fourteen*. A kid. Even if it *was* a cry for help, she couldn't have expected you to recognise it, let alone know what to do about it.'

'You don't…blame me, then?'

'The only thing I'd blame you for is hiding it from me. Not telling me right from the start.'

'You were so gutted. I couldn't make it worse. I…love you, too, bro.'

Jake wished he was close enough to give Ben a hug. 'And let's agree to leave the bad stuff behind, okay? No more thinking the past is going to shape the future. We might be Charles Logan's sons but we're *nothing* like him.

You were wrong when you said that happy endings only belong in one of my movies. They can happen for real.'

'I know.' Ben sounded choked up. Good grief…was that a *sniffle* Jake heard?

'No more hiding,' he ordered, trying to keep his tone light. 'Put the truth out there and live with it. The people who love you will understand.'

'You're right.' Yep. Ben certainly sounded more emotional than Jake had ever heard him sound. 'I've done that, Jake. With Mary—the woman I'll love till the day I die. You're not going to believe this but…I'm getting married. Not only getting married but I'm going to be a father.'

'Holy heck…'

'I *can* do it. Love. Family. The whole shebang. So can you. Get the truth out there and see what happens. *Trust*.'

The truth?

The truth was that Jake loved Ellie and didn't want to spend another minute without her in his life if it could be helped.

There was still the small problem of finding a way to tell her.

Of even getting her to agree to see him. He might not be responsible for the way her trust in men had been shattered in the past but he'd still have to pick up those pieces as well as the contribution he'd made.

The route from the hotel gymnasium to his room took Jake past the reception desk and a souvenir shop, the window of which had a display of cute, fluffy, soft toy kiwis.

Jake stopped in his tracks, staring through the window.

Then he pulled out his phone and hit a number on his speed dial.

'Kirsty? How's it going in Queenstown? You having

a good break?' He listened for only a moment. 'Can you do me a big favour? As soon as you hang up, text me the number for the woman who runs the bird-rearing centre we took the baby kiwi to. Jillian? I need to talk to her.'

# CHAPTER TWELVE

For a moment Jillian hesitated before dialling the number she needed.

Was she doing the right thing—interfering in her friend's life like this? Jake had been very convincing, of course, but wasn't that part of why Ellie didn't believe she could trust him anymore—because he was capable of making people believe whatever he wanted them to believe?

No. It wasn't just that she was prepared to believe the best of people. Or that she didn't have the kind of tragedies and disappointments that Ellie had had in her life that made it harder for her to trust. This was a time when the wisdom of years counted. When you could see the big picture and more than a glimmer of hope that someone you loved so much might be able to find the happiness she deserved.

Waiting for the call to be answered, Jillian deliberately put a big smile on her face so that her voice wouldn't give away the secret she'd been keeping for days now. She'd be able to sound no more than excited.

'Ellie...I've got news.'

'Hi, Jill. Is it good news?'

'Sure is.' Jillian's smile widened. 'I've managed to track down the new owners of Half Moon Island. And we've got permission to release Pēpe there.'

'Oh...that's *fantastic* news. When?'

'As soon as it can be arranged. I'm onto it…but…' Jillian took a deep breath. 'Hang onto your hat, hon. That's not all.'

'Oh?'

'The new owners are really excited by the idea. So excited they're planning to turn Half Moon into an official bird sanctuary.'

She could hear Ellie's gasp. 'Have they got any idea how much that would *cost?*'

'I get the impression they're not short of funds. What they *are* short of, though, is expertise. They need to find someone who could set it up and keep it running. I said I might know someone who could be interested.'

There was a stunned silence on the other end of the line. And then Ellie's voice was no more than a whisper.

'You mean *me*…? Oh, Jill…That might be exactly what I need in my life right now.' Her voice grew stronger. 'Have you met the owners? Who are they? What are they like?'

'You can find out for yourself. I suggested that we meet for a drink. They're pretty busy, but are you free late on Thursday night? Say nine p.m.? I'm thinking somewhere local for you. One of those gorgeous little café bars in Devonport?'

'I'm free. Of course I'm free. Oh…I can't believe this is happening. Am I dreaming?'

Jillian laughed. 'No. You're not dreaming and neither am I but— I've got to go, hon. I think we've got a new arrival coming in. See you Thursday.'

Ending the call, Jillian looked through the window of her quiet office into an equally quiet area outside. Nobody was arriving, but she hadn't been sure how much longer she could keep the lid on her secret.

She closed her eyes. Her part was over.

It was up to Jake now.

And Ellie could still make her own choices. It wasn't really interfering, was it?

Just helping.

The timing was perfect.

Ellie had been dreading Thursday night ever since that invitation had arrived in the mail a few days ago.

An invitation to a private screening of the first cut of Jake's movie. There was still a lot of work to do, but the production crew was ready to get a feel for the whole movie and not just sections, and they wanted a big screen so they'd hired a small theatre. The venue was top secret so that there was no chance of anyone from the media sneaking in or someone trying to pirate the footage. Anyone who wanted to attend would have to ring Kirsty on the day to find out the location and time.

Ellie had been circling the problem, torn between a longing to see Jake again—even if it was only on a big screen—and not wanting to take such a huge step backwards in the programme of 'getting over Jake.'

Now she didn't have to fight the battle. Meeting the new owners of Half Moon Island and discussing what could be an entirely new future for herself was not only the sensible thing to do—it was the first time since things had ended with Jake that Ellie was feeling hopeful that life could still be good.

What did you wear to a meeting that might be such a huge turning point in life? Someone who was serious about bird conservation and was prepared to live in isolation on a tiny island wouldn't be interested in dressing up to the nines and they were only meeting in a casual bar, but Ellie still wanted to present herself well.

She'd lost weight recently so her jeans looked pretty good, especially since it was cool enough in the evenings now to tuck them into long boots. Something for warmth was needed over her pretty top but when Ellie pulled out her favourite long shawl cardigan, she had to fight back sudden tears.

This was the cardigan she'd worn on that first night on set. When she'd gone for that walk on the beach with Jake and he'd shared secrets with her because he trusted her.

The night he'd kissed her and she'd known there was no point in trying to deny that she was in love with him.

The soft wool felt warm and comforting as she buried her face in it. Could she bear to wear it again? This might be the real test. If she could wear an item of clothing that almost had the smell of Jake on it and still step forward into a new future she would know that everything would be all right. That she could survive.

By the time she'd stepped off this particular ride on her emotional roller-coaster, Ellie was running late. With no time to braid her hair, she simply brushed it, grabbed her bag and headed out to meet Jillian. At least the meeting point was within easy walking distance.

'Which bar are we going to?' she asked, having greeted her friend.

'Come with me. It's not far.'

Ellie knew this area like the back of her hand, but she had no idea where they were going as Jillian ducked down a side street, into a driveway and past a row of rubbish bins to a very unassuming wooden doorway. Oddly, a man who looked like a bouncer was standing outside. Even more oddly, he gave Jillian a nod and opened the door that led into a long, narrow and very dark corridor.

'Where on *earth* are you taking me?'

'Shhh...' Jillian held a warning finger against her lips and Ellie was startled enough to fall silent.

And then she heard them. Voices. And one of those

voices was someone she knew so well that the sound entered every cell in her body and took her breath away.

Jake's voice. So loud and clear it could only be a recording.

She would have stopped in her tracks. Turned around and fled even, but Jillian was blocking any escape route. Urging her forward. And suddenly Ellie found herself in the back of the small theatre, having come through a curtain screening one of the emergency exits.

And now she couldn't have moved even if Jillian had tried to force her. The screen was huge and it was filled with Jake's face. The room was resonating to the sound of his voice. It was the first time Ellie had seen him on a big screen and the effect was totally overwhelming. She shrank back into the folds of the curtain, trying desperately to get a grip on such a larger-than-life experience. To cope with the wash of such an overwhelming rush of emotion.

The comfortable, plush seats of the theatre were full of people, but they were all riveted by what was happening on screen. Apparently nobody had seen Jillian and Ellie sneak in and while she was appalled at how her evening had been hijacked, there was nothing she could do for the moment. And they were standing near the back. It would be possible to slip out before the lights came back on and nobody would even have to know she'd been here. It wouldn't be for very long either, because they'd come in quite close to the end.

Jake was busy saving Amber. How had they managed to get such good close-up footage of him making the dangerous jump off the ship into the sea with Amber in his arms, without revealing that it was a stunt double he was carrying?

Watching him walk out of the surf with those wet clothes clinging to his body was almost too much. Ellie's hands clutched a fold of the velvet curtain beside her and crushed it into her palm.

The cardigan wasn't the real test of her resolve, was it? Not even close. *This* was going to be the real test. Having to listen to Jake say those lines again. The lines he'd deceived her with. Ellie steeled herself and willed them to happen because they would hurt all over again and they'd make her angry and get rid of any doubts she might be harbouring that she'd done the right thing in walking away.

And it was so much clearer. Not just bigger. The cameras had gone in for a very close shot as Jake was speaking and it was a perspective that she couldn't possibly have had, seeing it in real life.

Dear Lord…she actually got to see the very pores of his skin and every minute twitch of muscles as he spoke the lines. To see right into his eyes. Those beautiful, dark gray eyes.

Except…something felt wrong.

Ellie had the curious sensation that her body was simply vanishing as she concentrated so hard on the screen, trying to figure out what was so discordant between what she was registering on screen and what was happening in her head. It was almost as if she was floating…getting closer and closer to the screen and those enormous eyes.

And then, with a blinding thump, well after the lines had finished and the scene was racing forward as Jake stepped through the portal and back to real time, she realised exactly what it was.

What was missing.

Jake's eyes hadn't looked anything like that when he'd said those words to her. They'd been so much more…alive.

Genuine?

Ellie was gripping the curtain again, but this time it

was to help her stay on her feet because the realisation was enough to make her feel dizzy.

Okay…the lines *were* part of a script and Jake had rehearsed them enough to have them well tucked into his memory so that he could produce them perfectly on screen.

But he had been acting when he'd used those lines in the movie.

He *hadn't* been acting when he'd said them to her. He'd meant every single word.

He *could* see his future in her eyes.

And he *had* been scared.

And what had she done when he'd made himself so vulnerable? She'd hit back and thrown everything away.

Any thoughts of escaping before Jake could see that she was here drained away. This might be the last chance she ever had to say something to the man she had loved and lost.

Still loved.

The very least she could try and do was to apologise. She owed it to Jake to let him know that he hadn't deserved the way she had treated him. Not that she would expect a mere apology to put things right but surely it would be better for both of them to make at least a kind of peace with which to move forward?

She was here.

He'd seen the two women slip in through the emergency exit because he'd been watching for it. He'd barely focused on the majority of the movie until then. It was even harder to try now.

Despite the darkness of the theatre, there had been more than enough light coming from the screen to reveal that Ellie's hair was flowing loose and Jake's hands itched to bury themselves in that cascade of silk again. And she was wearing *that* cardigan. The one she'd worn that evening when they'd paddled in the sea. When he'd known he was with someone he felt totally safe with.

But if focusing on the movie was hard then, he knew it would be nothing compared to having to watch *that* scene. He would never be able to watch that without cringing. It was all too easy to put himself in Ellie's place and imagine how she must have felt, learning that his apparently heartfelt declaration had been nothing more than rehearsed lines.

It was so hard not to turn his head again, but if Ellie knew that he knew she was here, she might simply vanish again and he wouldn't have the chance to say what he wanted to say so much. He could only hope that she wouldn't see all this as being stage-managed. Fake. That maybe she would understand that desperate times called for desperate measures.

The clapping and cheering of all the people still involved with the movie, or staying on in New Zealand to have a holiday, faded as the massive curtains settled back into place in front of the screen and Steve stepped up onto the stage to say how happy he was with the way the movie had come together and thank everyone for all their hard work.

'Drinks and supper will be served in a few minutes,' he finished, 'but I know you're all waiting to hear a few words from the star of the show. So here's Jake...'

He'd never been this nervous giving a speech in public. His heart had never thumped this hard or his mouth been this dry. Jake didn't dare look to see if Ellie was still there, shrouded by the curtain. Not yet anyway.

'Obviously, I want to echo Steve's thanks to you all,' he began. 'It's not only a great movie but I've had the best time of my life making it. Acting's the best job in the world

because—for a while—you get to play—to live the fantasies that most people can only dream about.'

He swallowed hard. 'Maybe the lines between reality
and fantasy get a bit blurred now and then, but I want you
to know that *I* know what's real.' He took a deep breath
and allowed his head to turn slowly until he was looking
straight at Ellie.

'What's worth fighting for.'

Her gasp was involuntary.

He had to have known she was there all along for his
gaze to find her so unerringly as he said those words. She
hadn't been able to take her eyes off him. He looked so
different, with his hair short and only a dark shadowing on
his jaw as a faded echo of that beard. She wanted to bury
her fingers in his hair. Stroke the outline of that strong jaw
and then leave kisses in the trail her fingers had made.

Shocked out of where her thoughts had been drifting,
Ellie tried to cling to that gaze but Jake looked away. Let
his gaze rove over everybody present.

'It's been a real privilege to spend time in New Zealand and I have to say I've fallen in love with kiwis. One
in particular anyway.'

Ellie's head was spinning. Was he talking about Pēpe?
Or *her?* And why on earth was he doing this in public?

A somewhat panicked scan of the theatre reassured Ellie
that she knew most of the people here and that she could
feel safe as part of the family that the cast and crew of
the movie represented, but this was still a huge step into
a space between something private and something that
would be on display for the whole world. Jake couldn't
know that what he was saying wasn't going to be leaked
to the media.

And this was…*real.*

With her new-found ability to see the difference, Ellie could read Jake's body language and hear it in the tone of his voice. It felt like she had suddenly become fluent in a new language.

She could speak Jake.

And fear had been replaced by trust.

He might be an amazing actor but Ellie could see the difference between the acting and reality now. So clearly, even a tiny flashback to the lines he'd given the media about their relationship meaning nothing made her cringe inwardly. How could she have believed—even for an instant—in something that was such obvious acting?

Did other people ever find a connection like this? On a level so deep that it felt like something vital in her very soul could see its own reflection in Jake's?

To love someone this much was terrifying.

Especially when she couldn't know where this was going or what Jake was going to say next.

Those words only confused her even more.

'I have a new project,' Jake said. 'I want to give this kiwi a home. Security for the rest of her life. Love.'

Jillian nudged Ellie and leaned close to whisper. 'Did I tell you that the feather test results came through? Pēpe's a girl.'

No. She hadn't passed on the news. He was talking about the baby bird, then. So why was her heart thumping so hard and so fast that Ellie thought she might pass out?

'This special kiwi has given me a new direction,' Jake continued. 'As some of you know, I've been looking at taking my career in a new direction. The Logan brothers' company funds wildlife projects and I intend to start filming and fronting documentaries about them. To try and do my bit, I guess, to make the world a slightly better place.'

The clapping was appreciative and encouraging, but

Ellie couldn't join in. Her hands wouldn't move. Her body was frozen. She had that odd, floaty feeling again.

'Acting has taught me a great deal,' Jake told everybody then. 'And maybe I've learned that the most important lesson is the value of *not* acting. Of being able to be myself.'

He was looking at Ellie again. So intently that other heads began to turn as well, but it didn't matter. The only thing that mattered was the next thing that Jake was going to say.

'And I've heard tell that you don't go looking for the person you want to live with for the rest of your life.' His voice was soft but it still carried in a silence that felt as if everybody in the theatre was holding their breath. 'You go looking for the person you can't live without.'

Everybody was staring at Ellie now.

What had she said to him that time? That if this was real then other people would have to find out some time?

This was that time. She couldn't be the only person here who could feel the electricity in this room. A current that was adding a delicious kind of buzz to that floating sensation.

'I've found that person,' Jake said, raw emotion making his voice a little hoarse. 'My kiwi.'

The trust being put on public display was breathtaking. From a man who'd been humiliated in public by a woman before, it was courageous to say the least. He couldn't know whether he was safe. He'd put his vulnerability into her hands once before and she'd trampled on it. Not only was he prepared to trust her again—in front of all these people and potentially in front of the whole world—he was trusting what they had found between them.

That connection. And a love that was strong enough to last the distance.

The rest of their lives.

Was Jake the person *she* couldn't live without?

Oh…there was absolutely no doubt about that.

Suddenly Ellie's body could move again, although her legs felt distinctly wobbly. She didn't have to think about where to move because there was only one direction she could possibly go.

Judging by the crescendo of applause and cheering as she floated towards the stage to join Jake, everybody else thought exactly the same thing.

They belonged together.

It was surprisingly easy to escape the champagne supper after the first wave of congratulations had been made.

Using the same emergency exit that Jillian had tricked Ellie into entering the theatre by, Jake took her out into the night to walk down to a tiny beach near the marina where the moonlight filled the sea with flashing diamonds of light.

Not that they could compete with the flash of the diamond Jake produced from his pocket.

'You can change it if you don't like it.' He smiled. 'But I couldn't ask you to marry me without having something to put on your finger.'

'I love it,' Ellie said. 'I love *you*. I think I have, ever since you carried me along that beach into the teeth of a cyclone.'

'And I think I started to fall in love with you when you gave me your hair tie.'

Ellie made a face. 'Wasn't much of a gift.'

'But I already knew how brave and amazing you were. When I saw you sitting there in front of the fire with that glorious hair all free—like it is now…' Jake's fingers wove themselves into her hair. 'That was when I realised you were incredibly beautiful as well. I might not have known it then, but I was already lost.'

'And I should have known I was lost when you went down into the hole to rescue Pēpe just for me.'

There was no more talking for some time then. They sat, side by side on the top of a rock wall, sharing magically tender kisses under the moonlight.

'I've missed you so much,' Jake whispered. 'It's only been days but I feel like I've wasted half my life.'

'Me, too.'

'We'll never let that happen again. Wherever we need to go, let's do it together. Even if we have to drag half a dozen kids with us to a hut in a wildlife park in Africa or a lighthouse in a bird sanctuary on Half Moon Island.'

Ellie's jaw dropped. 'Oh...*no*. I totally forgot. I was supposed to be meeting the new owners of Half Moon Island tonight. Or was that just a trick of Jill's to get me to the theatre?'

'It wasn't and you have.'

Ellie laughed. 'Fire that scriptwriter,' she said. 'I didn't understand a word of that.'

The flash in Jake's eyes was fierce. 'It's not a script,' he said. 'And it never will be, between us. Even if the words happen to be the same. This...this is as *real* as it gets. The truth and nothing but the truth, okay?'

Ellie could only nod. Her heart was so full it hurt.

'Always.' Her smile wobbled. 'But I still didn't understand.'

'Jill's been a rock,' Jake told her. 'She knew how I felt about you and she gave me hope. She also put me in touch with some other people. The paperwork's not through yet, but you've met the new owner of Half Moon Island. It's me. Us.'

The gift was priceless. Because of the memories. Because it was already a part of her soul.

'And…and you're serious about turning it into a sanctuary?'

'Couldn't be more serious. And not just a sanctuary for birds. I'm hoping it will be a sanctuary for us, too. We could do up the cottage, couldn't we? Put in a proper helipad and boat ramp and go there whenever we need time just for ourselves? A place that couldn't be more private?'

To always be able to go back to the first place they'd made love? Blessed by the memories of the other people in her life that she had loved and been loved by? Ellie couldn't stop the tears filling her eyes and her chest being too tight to speak, but it didn't matter. She could simply kiss Jake until she found her voice again.

'That would be…just perfect.'

'You know what else would be perfect?'

'What?'

'If we could get married there.'

# EPILOGUE

IT *WAS* THE perfect place for a wedding.

Okay, the logistics had been a bit challenging, but they were getting used to that now, after months of ferrying tradesmen and materials to the tiny island. But given that it was a ceremony half the world seemed to want to watch and that the stars of this particular scene wanted to keep it as private as possible, the isolated venue couldn't have been better.

They weren't shutting the world out completely. The important people in their lives were here. An off-duty rescue helicopter, which had brought Dave and Mike and Smithie and their partners, was sharing the helipad with the sleek black machine that Ellie intended to learn to fly herself because Jake had claimed the captain's duties for their yacht.

There was company for that yacht down at the new jetty, too. Steve and Kirsty and others from the movie crowd had come by boat and Ben and his new wife, Mary, had been excited to try out their new yacht—a gorgeous replacement for the one wrecked in that long-ago storm.

As she took a last peep through the window of the cottage, Ellie could see the brothers standing side by side outside the white, open-sided marquee that had been erected on the newly mown grass beneath the lighthouse. They weren't identical twins, but they were equally tall and gorgeous-looking and they were wearing the same elegant gray suits with the flash of red from the posy of pohutu-kawa flowers in their buttonholes.

She saw them exchange a glance and smile at each other. She saw Ben squeeze his brother's shoulder as Jake cast a hopeful look towards the doorway through which his bride would emerge. He had to shade his eyes against the glare of the summer sunshine. The marquee had been an insurance policy against helicopters and cameras with telephoto lenses, but the shade it provided was going to be a bonus on this stunning day with its clear blue sky and calm seas.

The conditions couldn't be more different from when Ellie had first met Jake. And Ben, come to think of it, when the brothers had been fighting over who was going to be rescued first.

Who could have dreamed that that storm would have changed the futures of both the Logan brothers? Not only because they'd both found new happiness and life partners but because, in the end, the rift between them had been healed and they were now closer than ever.

She saw the brothers turn and enter the shade beneath the marquee. They would all be waiting for the bride and matron of honour to arrive now.

'You look gorgeous. I don't think I've ever seen you wearing a dress, but that is absolutely perfect on you.'

'Thanks, Jill.' Ellie smoothed the raw silk of the sheath dress that fitted like a glove until it flared out from knee level. How long would it take Jake to see the private mes-sage in the beadwork on the bodice and cap sleeves? Subtle shades of white and cream in the tiny pearl beads had lent themselves to a discreet repeating pattern.

Yin and yang. Two halves creating a whole.

Not just for twins.

For herself and Jake now.

She picked up her bouquet. The main flush of red blooms from New Zealand's native Christmas tree was well over, but they flowered a little later out here on Half Moon Island and it hadn't been hard to find enough to accompany the white roses. More of the feathery red flowers were clipped into the twist of hair that was supposed to make Ellie's loose hair behave in the sea breeze.

Jillian's youngest granddaughter, Charlotte, was holding a basket of red and white rose petals.

'Can we go now?' she begged. 'I want to throw the petals.'

Jillian smiled at Ellie. 'You ready, hon?'

'I can't wait. I'll be right behind you.'

Jillian took Charlotte's hand and moved towards the door. 'Don't start throwing until we're under the tent. We don't want to run out of petals, do we?'

Stepping outside, Ellie looked up at the lighthouse.

Tears blurred her eyes for a heartbeat as she gathered the memories of her family around her.

'I so wish you were all here,' she whispered. 'Grandpa and Mum and Dad—I hope you know how happy I am. And how much we love this place. We're going to take such good care of it, I promise.'

Jake had seen this lighthouse as a symbol of both danger and safety.

Ellie could only see the safety. A strong, silent sentinel that was always going to be there to help bring people home safely.

Gathering her skirt in her hands, Ellie moved towards the marquee.

*She* was going home.

Because that was where the heart was, wasn't it?

It wouldn't matter where in the world she and Jake were, she would always be home because she would be with the man she would love for the rest of her life.

She paused again before she stepped onto the trail of rose petals Charlotte had created to lead her through the centre of the intimate gathering.

Just for a moment.

So that she could bask in the expression on Jake's face when he saw her. The admiration. The love. The promise...

And then she walked forward. Past smiling faces and murmurs of appreciation. Past where Mary was sitting with the cocoons that held her and Ben's newborn twins.

Tears threatened to blur her vision again then. She would never forget the look in Jake's eyes when he'd met his tiny niece and nephew for the first time a couple of days ago.

He'd caught her gaze and held it and she'd seen the same kind of wonder she'd seen when they'd been watching Pēpe hatch. And more...she'd seen his hopes and dreams for their own future family. She'd seen the love that would be there for all of them.

For ever.

That look was there again as she reached his side, handing her bouquet to Jillian so that she could link hands with Jake in front of the celebrant.

For a long, long moment, however, they could only look at each other.

Sharing vows in public was merely a formality. Those vows had already been made and were locked in place for ever. Their hopes and dreams were the same.

And it would happen.

Sooner than Jake might expect.

Later, when everyone had gone, they could go back to their secret place. Even more special now because it was where the burrow had been made for Pēpe's new home, it had been used more than once to share their love.

It would be the perfect place to tell him that he was going to become a father.

* * * * *

# Mills & Boon® Hardback
## July 2014

# ROMANCE

| | |
|---|---|
| Christakis's Rebellious Wife | Lynne Graham |
| At No Man's Command | Melanie Milburne |
| Carrying the Sheikh's Heir | Lynn Raye Harris |
| Bound by the Italian's Contract | Janette Kenny |
| Dante's Unexpected Legacy | Catherine George |
| A Deal with Demakis | Tara Pammi |
| The Ultimate Playboy | Maya Blake |
| Socialite's Gamble | Michelle Conder |
| Her Hottest Summer Yet | Ally Blake |
| Who's Afraid of the Big Bad Boss? | Nina Harrington |
| If Only... | Tanya Wright |
| Only the Brave Try Ballet | Stefanie London |
| Her Irresistible Protector | Michelle Douglas |
| The Maverick Millionaire | Alison Roberts |
| The Return of the Rebel | Jennifer Faye |
| The Tycoon and the Wedding Planner | Kandy Shepherd |
| The Accidental Daddy | Meredith Webber |
| Pregnant with the Soldier's Son | Amy Ruttan |

# MEDICAL

| | |
|---|---|
| 200 Harley Street: The Shameless Maverick | Louisa George |
| 200 Harley Street: The Tortured Hero | Amy Andrews |
| A Home for the Hot-Shot Doc | Dianne Drake |
| A Doctor's Confession | Dianne Drake |

0614GEN STD HB

# Mills & Boon® Large Print
## July 2014

## ROMANCE

| | |
|---|---|
| A Prize Beyond Jewels | Carole Mortimer |
| A Queen for the Taking? | Kate Hewitt |
| Pretender to the Throne | Maisey Yates |
| An Exception to His Rule | Lindsay Armstrong |
| The Sheikh's Last Seduction | Jennie Lucas |
| Enthralled by Moretti | Cathy Williams |
| The Woman Sent to Tame Him | Victoria Parker |
| The Plus-One Agreement | Charlotte Phillips |
| Awakened By His Touch | Nikki Logan |
| Road Trip with the Eligible Bachelor | Michelle Douglas |
| Safe in the Tycoon's Arms | Jennifer Faye |

## HISTORICAL

| | |
|---|---|
| The Fall of a Saint | Christine Merrill |
| At the Highwayman's Pleasure | Sarah Mallory |
| Mishap Marriage | Helen Dickson |
| Secrets at Court | Blythe Gifford |
| The Rebel Captain's Royalist Bride | Anne Herries |

## MEDICAL

| | |
|---|---|
| Her Hard to Resist Husband | Tina Beckett |
| The Rebel Doc Who Stole Her Heart | Susan Carlisle |
| From Duty to Daddy | Sue MacKay |
| Changed by His Son's Smile | Robin Gianna |
| Mr Right All Along | Jennifer Taylor |
| Her Miracle Twins | Margaret Barker |

0614 GEN STD LP

# *Mills & Boon® Hardback*
## *August 2014*

## ROMANCE

| | |
|---|---|
| **Zarif's Convenient Queen** | Lynne Graham |
| **Uncovering Her Nine Month Secret** | Jennie Lucas |
| **His Forbidden Diamond** | Susan Stephens |
| **Undone by the Sultan's Touch** | Caitlin Crews |
| **The Argentinian's Demand** | Cathy Williams |
| **Taming the Notorious Sicilian** | Michelle Smart |
| **The Ultimate Seduction** | Dani Collins |
| **Billionaire's Secret** | Chantelle Shaw |
| **The Heat of the Night** | Amy Andrews |
| **The Morning After the Night Before** | Nikki Logan |
| **Here Comes the Bridesmaid** | Avril Tremayne |
| **How to Bag a Billionaire** | Nina Milne |
| **The Rebel and the Heiress** | Michelle Douglas |
| **Not Just a Convenient Marriage** | Lucy Gordon |
| **A Groom Worth Waiting For** | Sophie Pembroke |
| **Crown Prince, Pregnant Bride** | Kate Hardy |
| **Daring to Date Her Boss** | Joanna Neil |
| **A Doctor to Heal Her Heart** | Annie Claydon |

## MEDICAL

| | |
|---|---|
| **Tempted by Her Boss** | Scarlet Wilson |
| **His Girl From Nowhere** | Tina Beckett |
| **Falling For Dr Dimitriou** | Anne Fraser |
| **Return of Dr Irresistible** | Amalie Berlin |

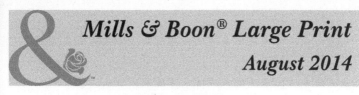

# Mills & Boon® Large Print
## August 2014

# ROMANCE

| | |
|---|---|
| A D'Angelo Like No Other | Carole Mortimer |
| Seduced by the Sultan | Sharon Kendrick |
| When Christakos Meets His Match | Abby Green |
| The Purest of Diamonds? | Susan Stephens |
| Secrets of a Bollywood Marriage | Susanna Carr |
| What the Greek's Money Can't Buy | Maya Blake |
| The Last Prince of Dahaar | Tara Pammi |
| The Secret Ingredient | Nina Harrington |
| Stolen Kiss From a Prince | Teresa Carpenter |
| Behind the Film Star's Smile | Kate Hardy |
| The Return of Mrs Jones | Jessica Gilmore |

# HISTORICAL

| | |
|---|---|
| Unlacing Lady Thea | Louise Allen |
| The Wedding Ring Quest | Carla Kelly |
| London's Most Wanted Rake | Bronwyn Scott |
| Scandal at Greystone Manor | Mary Nichols |
| Rescued from Ruin | Georgie Lee |

# MEDICAL

| | |
|---|---|
| Tempted by Dr Morales | Carol Marinelli |
| The Accidental Romeo | Carol Marinelli |
| The Honourable Army Doc | Emily Forbes |
| A Doctor to Remember | Joanna Neil |
| Melting the Ice Queen's Heart | Amy Ruttan |
| Resisting Her Ex's Touch | Amber McKenzie |

Discover more romance at

# www.millsandboon.co.uk

- ❤ WIN great prizes in our exclusive competitions

- ❤ BUY new titles before they hit the shops

- ❤ BROWSE new books and REVIEW your favourites

- ❤ SAVE on new books with the Mills & Boon® Bookclub™

- ❤ DISCOVER new authors

PLUS, to chat about your favourite reads, get the latest news and find special offers:

- 🔲 Find us on facebook.com/millsandboon
- 🐦 Follow us on twitter.com/millsandboonuk
- ❤ Sign up to our newsletter at millsandboon.co.uk